A BROOKHAVEN PARANORMAL COZY MYSTERY
BOOK 6

# HIGH SPIRITS

## S.E. BIGLOW

If you enjoy this work, please consider leaving a review.

For information contact; www.sarah-biglow.com

Edited by Under Wraps Publishing

Cover Design by: Deranged Doctor Design

Print ISBN: 978-1-955988-37-7

Published by S.E. Biglow: August 2024

10 9 8 7 6 5 4 3 2 1

# SPECIAL THANKS

I would like to thank all of the wonderful backers who supported this series on Kickstarter and made these books possible.

I need to give an extra special shout out to Jean Sitkei, Monica Kim, Anonymous Reader, Anonymous, Kathryn, Sara Vath, jeffrey.tristan.thyme, Ryan Scott James, GhostCat, Louisa, Rebecca Carter, Tory Penfield, Margaret M. St. John, Chloe Campbell, Heiko Koenig, Tom S., Alexandra Corrsin, Francesco Tehrani, maileguy, Rosie Pease, Sketch, Ernie Ridley, Amelia Pluck, Ayl, John Idlor, Sandy K., Brian D. Lambert, Michelle Kaye, Bonniejean Boettcher, Nicole Valdez, Eva S., Megan, Voldane Pelt, Diane Wagoner, Katrina, Rebecca Bock, Karin Baxter, Krista abd Barbara Griffiths, Jennifer Herschbach, Lisa Spalding, Sam, Isaac Dansicker, PippiMD, Brian, Rayne Sinclair, Mike Jones, Katie, Cheryl, Leslie, Nicole, Melissa, Vi Ta, Beth Caudill, Jennifer

Preslar, Sasha Washburn, Matthew Walker, Jackie Ewing, Jenna N., Stephen Ballentine, Melissa Showers and Rob Steinberger

1
———

$\mathcal{A}$utumn settled over Brookhaven as I marked my first full year as a Brookhaven resident. This year, the leaves had turned by the start of October and littered the sidewalks by the middle of the month. Maybe it was childish of me, but I'd delighted in racing through the foliage, feeling it crunch beneath my feet. The air had turned crisp and biting in the mornings. Yet it still held the promise of new life that would be back before we knew it. With only a few days until Halloween, everyone in town was consumed with preparations for the All Hallows Eve Extravaganza. Businesses from all around town lined Main Street in an open-air market, selling their wares and generally celebrating the season.

The Extravaganza was an annual event. But this time I truly felt part of the festivities. Last year, I'd hardly known anyone beyond Tania and Maggie. Now though, people knew me. I'd proven myself to be dedicated to protecting Brookhaven and keeping its residents safe. Plus, Sage had put me in charge of High Time's booth since she was out of town.

"This is a big responsibility," Maggie said as she helped me load the last box of decorations into the back of Tania's VW Bug.

"If I'm honest, I wouldn't be my first choice. I'm just the woman who tends the plants. I don't interface with customers and there are plenty of people who've been around longer than me," I replied, voicing my doubt about Sage's choice.

"But you're likable and whether you realize it or not, you have a calming effect on people," my girlfriend said, leaning over to plant a kiss on my lips.

It wasn't just people I appeared to have an effect on. Over the last few months, the plants we cultivated at High Time appeared to respond more to my temperament. They grew like wildfire when I was in a good mood and verged on wilting if I was in a bad mood.

"I think the more comfortable I become here, the more my magic is seeping into people and things around me," I confided. "Maybe it's my magic they feel they're connecting with?"

"Well, is that a bad thing? Your magic is just as much a part of you as your sparkling personality. And you deserve to be celebrated," Maggie said, shutting the back door and climbing into the passenger seat of the car.

"This is a crazy idea. But I've been thinking, what if I told people I'm a witch?" I broached as I climbed behind the wheel.

"Oh ... Like coming out?" Maggie answered with an arched brow.

"Yeah. I mean, it isn't exactly a secret around here that magic is real. Vinnie and Chief Hayes know the truth. And so does Ginny and half a dozen other people. Why shouldn't I just be fully open about it?"

"It's a bold move. I'm not even fully out at the clinic," Maggie admitted, reaching for my hand. "But if you're ready to come out, I'm here to support you every step of the way. Just tell me what you need."

I gave her outstretched hand a squeeze. "I hadn't gotten that far, yet. It's just something I've been thinking about for a while."

In truth, it had been something rolling around in the recesses of my mind since Tania's abduction in

July. I couldn't quite explain why though. I had this nagging feeling that if I'd been open about my abilities it could have made a difference in how long Tania was forced to suffer at the hands of Dr. Elijah Fitz. A part of me acknowledged it was a foolish idea. My magical abilities being common knowledge wouldn't have stopped a vampire and his human accomplice from kidnapping my friend. Maybe it was my way of processing the guilt I felt from Tania having been swept up in the middle of his devious scheme.

The B&B had finally settled back into a sense of normalcy at the start of October. Despite being adamant that both Maggie and I were available to talk, Tania had chosen to process her trauma quietly and in private. Some days she hardly came out of her room at all. Even Sam and Beau had kept their distance.

"Darcy, where'd you go?" Maggie's voice jolted me from the trip down memory lane.

"Sorry. Just thinking about Tania."

"She's been doing better lately." It came out more like a question than a statement of fact.

"I just hate that she felt she couldn't lean on us."

"Everyone processes things differently. And I'm

sure it helped her to know we were available if she really needed us."

"I know. But it still doesn't stop me from feeling like I failed my friend."

"Enough doom and gloom. The Extravaganza is meant to be a party," Maggie prompted.

I nodded and put the car in drive, leaving High Time in the rearview mirror. I paralleled the board-walk across Main Street and pulled into the alley that ran behind most of the shops on the thorough-fare. I managed to squeeze the VW Bug into a spot right behind Ginny's. Not surprisingly, the café had become the headquarters of the festivities. All of the shops and their vendor designees were set to meet for a final walk through before the event started on the day before Halloween.

Maggie and I left the car full of decorations and made our way around to the entrances of the store-fronts. The street had been cordoned off on both ends to allow for the stalls to be set up. Public Works employees were scattered along the street as they wrangled tents and tables. Excitement permeated the atmosphere as I led the way into the café, the bell above the door announcing our arrival.

"You're late," Ginny said, spotting us.

"Sorry," I said, taking a seat at the counter.

Her usual place of honor—the middle stool—remained empty even though a dozen other shop owners crammed in around the counter. Ginny stood on the opposite side, an easel with a diagram of Main Street propped up behind her. Each tent was marked by a number that corresponded to a legend along the far right. It appeared High Time was only one booth down from where Ginny would be selling her café goods.

I looked around to see how many of the other merchants I recognized. The head librarian was at one end of the counter, seated beside the lead editor of the local paper. On the far end, I did a double take when I spotted Tyson, the town's pawn shop proprietor, leaning against a table. I had never seen the man outside of his shop. Part of me had wondered whether he was bound to the space somehow. I knew Ginny had helped him with some magic that forced customers to only tell the truth in his shop. As far as I knew, he wasn't magical himself.

"Now that everyone is accounted for, we're going to run through logistics," Ginny called, drawing attention to herself.

Quiet fell over the space as Chief Hayes stepped up to stand shoulder-to-shoulder with his sister. It wasn't the first time I'd seen them in close proximity to one another. Only in the bright lighting of the café's interior, I could see just how much they resembled one another, from their blond hair to the shape of their face and the way they carried themselves with such confidence. The only thing that really set them apart was the odd amber glint in the chief's eyes.

"For a lot of you this is going to be familiar, but for those of you just joining us," the chief stated as he gave me a pointed look, "we set up booths today. Festivities begin tomorrow at noon and run through nine o'clock on Halloween. While it's not an explicit requirement, the kids have come to expect treats from the booths on Halloween."

The way his jaw worked suggested he wanted to say more. That he was trying hard not to call me out to make sure we had some regular goodies to hand out. I had no intention of giving anything pot-laced to children.

"What about the bonfire?" the librarian interjected.

"Yeah. You aren't going to cancel it again, are you?" the editor implored, producing pen and paper as if to take notes for their next article.

From what I recalled, a lot of folks in town had been disappointed by its absence the year before.

Ginny cleared her throat and interjected. "We've just finished securing the location. We'll be holding it in the field behind Tyson's shop around eight o'clock. He graciously agreed to let us use his land."

I turned to Maggie. "Am I missing something about this bonfire? Why is it such a big deal?'

"For as long as I can remember, it's been part of the celebration. It's a way to honor those we've lost and celebrate the year ahead with the people still with us. For some people in town it holds spiritual significance."

"Sounds nice. Why didn't it happen last year?"

"Supposedly because they couldn't find a place to hold it. It's been on the boardwalk before, but a few years ago there was an incident where it got out of control," Maggie replied.

It sounded like the sort of thing that should happen as far from wooden structures as possible. So, having it out near Tyson's shop, and on the edge of town, seemed a smart move. Plus, it was easy to access from Main Street, which meant everyone could get from the tents to the bonfire and back without issue.

Chief Hayes cleared his throat, nudging his sister back so he could continue. "As Ginny said, the bonfire is back on this year. We will of course have both fire and medical staff on standby in case of emergencies. If you find you need such assistance at any other time, call the number on the top of the board here. It is my personal number."

I hastily added the chief's number to my contacts so I wouldn't forget it. It felt a little strange to have a direct line to the chief of police. Our relationship had softened over time. He didn't look at me with disdain and annoyance whenever our paths crossed anymore. He was even downright pleasant sometimes.

"If you need extra candy, I've got some stocked at the clinic," Maggie noted.

"Thanks. But Tania bought a bunch of bags for the B&B and said I could take some for the booth," I answered.

With the chief's number disseminated, the formal part of the gathering ended. Shop owners dispersed, some likely heading to begin tent set up. I wound my way around the edge of the counter to stand beside Tyson.

"It's very generous of you to offer your land for the bonfire," I told him.

"Some things are tradition," he replied with a shrug. "I see Sage has left you in charge during her absence."

"Thomas and a few others will help throughout the day," I explained, and glanced at the diagram still displayed behind the counter. "I see you've got a tent, too."

"I can accept items anywhere," he noted.

That statement surprised me. I knew that Tyson had been tricked once, which was why Ginny had given him the charm that compelled people entering his shop to only tell the truth. Did that extend to the tent? Had she given him a charm for this occasion to encourage him to get out of his shop?

"Well, I suppose that's true. I'm excited to really be in the thick of things this year," I said.

He gave me a quizzical look. "You know, the bonfire isn't just for honoring the dead. It's about celebrating your truth."

A shiver danced down my spine at his words. He knew I was a witch already, but could he sense what I was considering doing? And had he just given me the perfect place to do it? Given the excitement in the room when Ginny confirmed the bonfire would happen this year, I assumed most of the town would be in attendance.

"Is there a particular truth you think I should be sharing?" I probed.

"I am not the one who traffics in truth. Only a

beneficiary of it," he said, jutting his chin in Ginny's direction.

I glanced over my shoulder to see her in conversation with Chief Hayes. I turned back to Tyson. "I might have something to share with people. Thanks for letting me know the bonfire is a good place to do it."

I retraced my steps back to Maggie in time to overhear Chief Hayes tell Ginny, "This needs to go off without a hitch."

"You just let me handle it, okay, Rick? You do your job and I'll do mine."

Their tones held more tension than had been present earlier. The way Ginny held her shoulders stiff as she spoke was a definite shift in body language, too. Chalking it up to a sibling dispute, I turned my attention to my girlfriend.

"We ought to get started setting up. I promised Tania I'd be back before dinner to help pack the free lunches she's donating to the library tent."

I spotted Thomas and his roommate Dennis approaching from a few shops down and gave them a wave to let them know I'd seen them. They passed what used to be Beekman Family Butchery. Since Brian Beekman's arrest for illegally harvesting organs, the shop had been shuttered and the space was technically for sale. Somehow, I pushed the thought of Brian and his crimes from my mind.

"We've got boxes around back in the car," I told Thomas once he was within earshot.

"Sounds good," he replied, gesturing to the rolled up sign slung in a protective case over his shoulder. "We can start getting the tent set up."

"Divide and conquer. I like it," I said, relief washing over me that I had my co-worker's support. He could have easily resented me for Sage's decision to delegate, but he'd never been one to hold a grudge.

Maggie and I rounded the back of the shops again. I opened the passenger side door, easing out a couple of boxes of decorations for the booth. Thomas had agreed to stop by High Time in the morning to pick up the confections and the cash box. Given the pot in our offerings, Sage had made sure I understood we couldn't leave them here overnight. In short order, Maggie and I carried the decor to the tent which Public Works had constructed. Dennis and Thomas had already unfurled the High Time banner. Together, we strung battery-powered purple and orange strobe lights along the interior of the tent and draped festive paper marijuana leaves along the table's edge.

"Here, help me pull the flaps to keep everything covered overnight." Thomas addressed Dennis and the two men easily secured the front of the tent.

A couple of tents down, I spotted Ginny starting to set out her own wares. I doubted anyone would be foolish enough to steal packaged coffee from her tent. Even from this distance, I could tell she was still on edge. I didn't want to get involved with whatever drama had befallen the Hayes siblings, so I just offered her a cordial wave. She returned the gesture with a forced smile and I said a silent prayer that the Extravaganza went off without a hitch.

## 2

My mood brightened as I sauntered up the front walk of Tania's B&B. The natural foliage might be on its way out, but I'd still managed to coax the pumpkins we'd carved to thrive, glowing even without the aid of candlelight or flashlights stowed within their hollowed out cores. The pair of grinning jack-o-lanterns greeted me as I bounded up the front steps and into the foyer.

"Tania, are you in here?" I called, approaching the kitchen.

I expected the space to be filled with the heady scent of my landlady's delicious cooking. Instead, I caught a heavy scent of smoke. Picking up the pace, I rushed in to find dark plumes of smoke billowing from the oven. Just as I reached the center of the industrial space, the alarm overhead began blaring in a high-pitched wail. Coughing through the smoke, I yanked the oven door open and hastily grabbed a towel to pull out a tray of burnt cookies.

"*Dios mio!*" Tania exclaimed as she rushed in, trying to wave the smell away.

Leaving the baking tray atop the oven, I rushed to the back door. Flinging it open, I moved on to the windows in the hopes of circulating some fresh air into the space.

"What happened in here?" Sam materialized beside me. The smoky backdrop of the kitchen dampened the sparkle of his rhinestone-studded dinner jacket and matching teal slacks.

Tania let out a frustrated sigh. "I was so busy trying to get everything ready for the Extravaganza, I lost track of what I was doing ... now the cookies are ruined." She sunk into one of the chairs around the kitchen table and rested her head in her hands.

I pulled up a seat opposite her and reached for her hands to give them a comforting squeeze. "Take a breath, yeah? It's going to be all right."

Her hands shook beneath mine as she raised her head, looking at me. "I just don't want to let people down."

I nodded at the trays of food already sitting on the counter, waiting to be wrapped up. "So you won't have as many cookies as you planned. You're offering up more than just baked goods. And people are going to love it."

"Aren't I supposed to be the one talking sense into you and validating your feelings?" she asked with a half-smile on her lips.

"Just because you're an empath doesn't mean the rest of us can't pick up the slack now and again."

"I am sorry. I haven't been quite myself lately."

"You went through something none of us can fully understand. You don't owe anyone an apology," I reminded her.

She nodded in agreement—mostly to convince herself I suspected—and pulled her hands free. She stood and approached the platters on the counter. "Well, these aren't going to finish themselves."

By the time we finished parceling out the food and wrapping it into individual portions, the smoke from the burnt cookies had cleared the kitchen. With it gone, Tania's mood had brightened. She gave me a knowing smile as we stacked the last tray of food in the back seat of the VW Bug.

"You are really excited for this event," she noted.

"I guess I am. I'm a little nervous since Sage put

me in charge of High Time's tent, but I feel like I'm finally settling in and finding my place."

"You are going to do wonderfully."

"Thanks. And I'm also looking forward to the bonfire tomorrow night."

"Why is that?" Tania closed the passenger side door and fixed me with a curious expression.

"I told Maggie this earlier, but I have been thinking about coming out to everyone."

"Darcy, I do not think anyone would be surprised by that news."

"Oh, not about me being a lesbian," I said with a hiccup of laughter. "I meant about being a witch."

"Now that makes more sense," she said slowly. "It is a big step for you."

"I know it is. But I think I'm ready for it. I want people to know who I really am. And I know in my heart that this place drew me in, because it was somewhere I'd be able to do that."

"Letting your full freak flag fly. I'm proud of you," Sam chimed in as he popped into existence above the hood of the car.

"You should do whatever makes you happy and fulfilled," Tania said.

The way her lips parted suggested she had more

to say, but kept it to herself. That wasn't like her. Sam leaned over, picking up on her hesitation, too.

"You think it isn't a good idea?" I pressed.

"Of course I don't," she answered, again stopping short of saying more.

"There's something you're not saying," I pointed out.

"Darcy, you deserve to be happy and if admitting to everyone in town that you have magic brings you happiness, then absolutely you should do it. But be aware there can also be a downside to revealing that sort of truth."

"Like what?"

"People come to expect things from you; assume that because you have supernatural gifts, they are there for the taking ... for their benefit."

I wanted to tell my friend that she was full of it and Brookhaven wasn't like that. Yet I couldn't help picture the steady stream of people passing through Ginny's. I couldn't recall many times when she wasn't surrounded by people. I'd always assumed she simply drew people to her and got them to confess their secrets. Was it more complicated than that? Were they drawn to her simply because they thought she could give them something they craved?

"I help plants grow. That's not very exciting," I said in a weak attempt to counter her concerns.

"You do more than that," she retorted. "You don't just help them grow. You can make them do things. Also, you can see through them, and relive their memories."

I hadn't considered those skills. They'd only ever manifested when someone was in trouble. I took a moment to process Tania's words. She was right. Those sort of abilities could be abused or misused if I wasn't careful.

"I appreciate you wanting to make sure I don't get taken advantage of, Tania," I said, giving the older woman a hug. "I promise, I won't let it get out of hand. But I need to do this."

"We both know that me telling you to be careful wasn't ever going to stop you from doing it anyway," she said with a smirk. "Now, come inside. I think there are enough leftovers to make a nice stew for tonight."

Dinner was delicious. Even Sam looked more forlorn than usual at his inability to eat as he watched Tania and I sit side by side at the dining room table. I hadn't seen Beau all afternoon, but he'd been keeping to himself the last few weeks. Given his telepathic abilities, I suspected he, too, needed a bit of peace and solitude. I made a mental note to check on my reptilian companion in the morning before heading out to the Extravaganza.

"So, Tyson told me that people use the bonfire to come clean about things. What's the craziest thing someone's confessed during one of these things?"

"I think he was exaggerating—" Tania said.

"Oh, no, he most definitely wasn't. One year, probably a decade ago," Sam interrupted, floating beside me in a clearly gossiping pose, "this woman admitted to sleeping with her best friend's boyfriend. Things were thrown, and blood was drawn. It was quite the epic cat fight."

"Things like that don't happen anymore," Tania said.

"You never know. People get worked up on Halloween. Something in the air that just makes people bubble over with revelations," Sam said with a shrug.

"Well, let's hope it doesn't devolve into a brawl," I said. Pushing back from the table, I gathered mine and Tania's plates to take into the kitchen.

I was determined to share my truth with the town that had become my home. But I didn't need violence erupting as a result. I still had a day to sort out the exact details of how I planned to make the announcement, so maybe a good night's sleep would bring some clarity.

THERE WAS an excited energy in the B&B when I awoke the next morning. I found Tania in the kitchen humming to herself. The counters, which had still been a bit of a disaster the night before, were pristine again. I even spotted Beau lounging on the back of one of the chairs.

"It's nice to see you in such a good mood," I told Tania and took the plate of waffles she offered.

"I think I just needed to get back to doing what I love," she answered and flipped the burner to the 'off' position before joining me at the table.

I leaned over and gave Beau's head a little stroke with the back of one finger. "Nice to see you out and about, too, mate. You had me worried."

*'Needed space.'*

"I know. If you're up for it, I could use your company at the tent."

The proposal earned me a sideways look from Tania. "You know how Beau feels about groups of people."

"I didn't intend for him to do anything other

than just sit and look cute. I'll be out all day and I've missed spending time with him," I explained. I looked back to the chameleon. "Besides, people gravitate to animals and Beau is unique enough he might be a bigger draw to our tent," I said. I wasn't ashamed to admit wanting higher profits to validate Sage's confidence in my abilities.

*'Enjoy time together.'*

"That settles it. Beau will come along with me," I said, turning my attention to the plate of food in front of me.

I was careful not to get syrup on the flowing sleeves of my blouse. I wasn't usually one for Halloween, but Sage had insisted we dress up for the Extravaganza. So, I'd done a little digging in my closet and paid a visit to a thrift shop just outside town to put together an outfit that made it look as if I'd walked off the set of Practical Magic. Given the announcement I was intending to make, that felt appropriate.

"I'll go with you to drop off extra food," Tania commented after cleaning the waffle maker. She'd donned an elegant evening gown in a deep purple that bordered on a dark red toward the hem. A thick fur wrap lay over the back of her chair. The change in clothes almost made Tania glow, brightening to her pre-kidnapping self.

"I have a good feeling about today," I said, mentally putting good vibes out into the universe.

"Have you thought any more about your big announcement?" Sam's voice filtered in from the dining room.

"I'm definitely going to do it during the bonfire. I'll just go with the flow and see when an opportunity presents itself," I answered.

"I'll be there in solidarity," Sam said. The usual jovial edge to his tone disappeared, replaced with sincerity.

"I really appreciate the support from all of you," I said, giving my companions a grateful smile.

"You should eat before your food gets cold. Besides, you want to be ready when everyone shows up," Tania said in a mothering tone.

I tucked in, savoring every bite of the meal she'd prepared. Before long, we were both crammed into the VW Bug, and Beau perched on my shoulder as we headed to the center of town.

The air of excitement I'd felt permeating the B&B when I awoke was tenfold along Main Street. Leaving the car parked behind the shops, Tania and I carried the trays to the food tent situated at the far end of the street, closest to the library and newspaper. The editor rushed forward, relieving Tania of her platter of food.

"Here let me take those. You should get set up," Tania said, motioning for me to pass over the tray in my own hands.

I happily divested myself of the food, offered my friend a wave, and weaved my way back through the other vendors setting up to find High Time's tent. Thomas was already there with dreads hanging loose around his neck for once.

"Who's that?" He gestured in the direction of my left shoulder.

"This is Beau. He, uh, lives with Tania and I at the B&B. I figured he might enjoy the fresh air and everyone loves a cute animal."

"He can be our unofficial mascot," Thomas replied with a broad grin. "I love it."

Beau scurried down my outstretched arm and settled on the table between a tray of taffy and some mini brownies THomas had picked up from High Time. Beau's scales shifted from a more muted green to an earthy brown to blend in with his surroundings.

"Whoah!" Thomas exclaimed.

"He's good at hiding in plain sight. But I'm sure

once we've got some customers, he'll brighten right up," I said, addressing my chameleon friend as much as my co-worker.

Beau blinked once in my direction before focusing his attention on our surroundings. I gave him a quick stroke along the scales on his back before stepping behind the table and making certain the cash box was ready to go.

"Okay. You ready for this madness?" Thomas fixed me with another big grin as he rubbed his hands together.

I didn't want to tell him I had doubts that our little shop would see a ton of business over the next two days, but I didn't have the heart to dampen his spirits. Besides, I needed to think positive and put out good vibes into the universe, so that tonight's big reveal went as planned.

**3**

_______

To my surprise, the town turned out in droves as soon as the Extravaganza officially opened at noon. Beau brightened up, seeming to have a magnetic pull over the whole street. I hadn't stopped to count the cash box, but I could tell we'd sold more than I'd expected for the entire event.

"You know, if you want to check things out, I can cover our table for a while," Thomas said, gesturing toward the rest of the street filled with booths. Using creativity, he'd done his dreads up to look like he'd been struck by lightning and donned a singed t-shirt to complete the effect.

"But I don't want to abandon you," I protested.

He let out a chuckle. "Go and enjoy yourself, Darcy. Everyone deserves to have some fun today."

I stowed the money I'd been counting in the cash box and rounded the table, leaving Thomas behind. I felt Beau latch on to my arm as I passed. The sun was already on its downward descent toward evening as I strolled past each of the other vendors on Main Street. I scanned the crowds of people, hoping to spot Maggie or Tania among the browsers. While I got a lot of friendly smiles and waves as I passed, none of them were the people I was looking for.

"Hey, Darcy. You okay?" Vinnie's voice caught me off guard as I stood opposite the library's booth.

I spun to face the deputy. "Yeah, just looking at everything. I've been stuck behind a table all day."

"I know, I saw you earlier. Right now you look like you're a little lost."

"Honestly, I've been trying to find Maggie or Tania in all of this, but haven't spotted them. I don't know, I just feel like I want to experience this with them."

"I think I saw Tania down by Ginny's booth. I don't think I've seen Maggie though. Of course, that doesn't mean she's not around."

"I'm sure I'll find her eventually," I replied.

Just then, the radio on Vinnie's belt crackled. He turned his back to address the incoming call and I refocused my attention on the library booth's display.

"Can I help you find anything in particular?" the librarian asked, drawing my attention.

"Just browsing," I answered, picking up a small volume of poems. "How have things gone for you today?"

"A little slow, but I'm honestly just glad we've had anyone come by. We've actually taken quite a few donations."

"I suppose libraries are always in need of new books," I noted and held up the book of poetry. "You know what, I'll take this. I think my Nan would get a kick out of it."

"Five dollars, please."

I handed over the cash and waved her off when she tried to give me back my change. "Consider it a donation."

"Thanks."

I stowed the book under my arm and wandered back the way I'd come, stopping across from Ginny's tent. Too many people were scrambling to reach her for me to get close. But I spotted Tania among the crowd, standing beside Ginny. After a few minutes, the throng thinned enough for me to approach. The trays that had been filled with baked goods and branded coffee were barren. Ginny looked frazzled.

"Looks like you've made out like a bandit," I commented.

"Huh? Oh, yeah. I think we've actually sold out of everything I'd put together. We'll have to restock in the morning."Ginny glanced at her phone screen.

"Something wrong?" I pressed.

"I need to get over to Tyson's to help set up for the bonfire," Ginny answered.

"I can close up for you if you've run out of wares," Tania offered.

"Thanks. You're a lifesaver." Ginny pocketed her phone and darted around the table heading towards the bonfire.

"How are you doing?" I addressed Tania as I helped her stack empty trays one on top of the other and stow them behind the table.

"Fine."

"Will I see you at the bonfire?"

"I will be there," she answered and tugged the tent flaps down over the table to signal that the booth was closed. She looked at me. "Aren't you supposed to be at the High Time booth?"

"Thomas is covering for me," I replied, sensing a

hint of judgment in her tone that felt entirely unnecessary.

"Right."

"You know, I should probably get back. I'll see you tonight. If you see Maggie, let her know I'm looking for her."

Tania nodded and headed the opposite direction. I moved back through the crowds as the sky darkened above me. The street lights flickered on, casting warm orange globes of light along the sidewalks and street while I passed people heading the opposite direction. I made it back to the High Time tent just as the last light flipped on overhead.

"What'd you find?" Thomas asked as I rejoined him behind the table. Beau reclaimed his perch between the taffy and brownies.

"Just a book of poetry for my Nan. Ginny sold out of everything she'd brought for today."

"Not surprised," he replied with a snort.

"Can I touch him?" a little girl with sandy hair and wide-framed glasses asked as she approached our tent and gestured toward Beau.

"Sure. Be gentle though and make sure you pet along his scales—head to tail," I instructed.

She bent down and ran a fingertip along Beau's back. I watched as he leaned into the gesture. The way he shifted his weight and took a few steps closer made her giggle.

"Addie, there you are," a woman with matching hair and glasses called, rushing to grab at the girl's hand.

"She's all right," I said, not wanting the child to get in trouble. "She was just saying hello."

"You know you're not supposed to go off alone," the woman continued as if I hadn't spoken.

"I wanted to see the pretty dragon," Addie answered.

"Actually, he's a chameleon," I corrected. "His name is Beau. And he says thank you very much for coming to meet him."

"He does?" Her eyes went wide behind the lenses of her glasses.

"Mm-hmm. He told me so."

"He did?" Her voice modulated into a high squeal.

"He's a very special chameleon. If you listen really hard sometimes you can hear what he's thinking."

"That's so cool," she chirped.

I turned to Thomas and gestured for the bucket of non-pot laced treats I'd brought along. "Would you like one?"

Addie glanced at her mother. I made eye contact with the woman. "They're store bought, not one of our products."

Relief washed over the woman and her shoulders lowered. "You can take one."

Addie took her time looking through the bucket to find the perfect treat. Her mother turned her full attention on me, making sure she was in hand's reach of her daughter.

"Was there something else I could help you with?" I asked in my best customer service voice.

"I don't usually buy things like this. But a friend of my husband's told me, I should give it a try. And she said Sage comes highly recommended."

"Happy to help," I answered and surveyed the items we had left. At a glance I couldn't say what level of plant extract an item contained and Thomas was busy helping other customers so I couldn't ask for his expertise.

"I don't want anything too strong," the woman added.

I'd never tried to access the remnants of the plants I'd tended within the baked goods they were infused into or through packaging. But my powers had been growing, so I didn't see why I wouldn't be able to do it. I pressed a hand onto the tray of taffy and closed my eyes, reaching inward for the kernel of my magic that always ignited spells. It responded to my mental summoning and turned its attention toward the tray. At first I felt nothing as my magic searched out the residual plant matter.

'Seek your magic.'

Beau's words popped into my mind and it took me a moment to understand what he meant. After a beat, it made sense. The plant matter had been used, but I'd nurtured every leaf that went into the goods on this table. My magic didn't disappear simply because the plant had changed states of matter. I pushed past the plastic wrapping and other ingredients to touch the magic that had guided the plants to originally blossom.

I let out a sharp intake of breath as the magic welled up, washing over me. The taffy was much too strong. I pulled my hand away and reached for the brownie bites, repeating the same process, and released a sigh.

"I would try the brownies," I finally said and held out a package. "They contain the mildest thing we've got right now."

"Thank you," she said and handed over a twenty dollar bill.

I busied myself with getting her change as Addie

finally settled on a lollipop from the bucket. I handed the money to the woman. "Have a good rest of your day and have fun tomorrow."

"Bye," Addie said and gave Beau a wave.

"Not to jinx things, but I think Sage is going to put you in charge of this every year," Thomas said with a nudge to my shoulder once we were alone.

"I didn't do anything," I protested.

"I don't know. This is the most successful the table's been since we opened five years ago."

Before I could respond, I spotted Maggie making her way down the street. I rounded the table just as she reached us. "Hey, you," I greeted and leaned in for a kiss.

Maggie returned the gesture and reached to take my hand in hers. "How is it going?"

"According to Thomas, this is the best we've done in ages," I replied.

"Glad to hear it."

I leaned into her arm. "I also did something new. I was able to tell the potency of the plants used in the edibles, so I could give the right recommendation to a woman looking to buy something. It was like I traced my magic memory. Weird, but kind of cool too."

"Sounds like your powers are continuing to expand and change."

"Hmm ... wonder how long that's going to happen?" I left Thomas to shuttle the remaining goods back to High Time for the night and close up the tent.

"I don't think anyone knows," she answered. "Anyway, the bonfire's about to get started. Are you ready?"

"As I'll ever be."

THE AIR WAS thick with wood smoke from the fire when we approached. The flames were contained in a three-foot wide stone circle and rose nearly five feet in the air. Almost everyone from town stood clustered around the blaze. Tables had been set up with food and drinks, and by the way a few people staggered and listed, I deduced alcohol was involved.

"So, how am I supposed to do this exactly?" I asked Maggie as we headed for the food.

"I think Rick is going to make some sort of speech first and then people can just go up and share whatever they want," Maggie answered.

"And people actually listen?"

"I doubt everyone is going to pay attention. But give them a reason to remember, and they will."

I took stock of our surroundings in the darkened space. The bonfire illuminated the rest of the field, covered with short grass, on the verge of turning brown. We were far enough from the center of town that the buildings weren't visible, only the distant twinkling of streetlights suggested we were anywhere close to Main Street. I could work with that.

"Hope you don't wait too long for your coming out," Sam's voice chirped from behind me. Even though most people couldn't see him, Sam's outfit was bedecked with Halloween splendor. He'd donned a bright green suit with a yellow and purple tie. The cuffs and collar of the jacket sparkled with iridescent sequins and beads. Somehow he'd managed to apply eye shadow in a rich purple-blue that accented his tie perfectly.

"You have somewhere more important to be?" I quipped.

"Maybe."

"Well, I'm glad you're here to support me anyway."

Just then, the sound of a microphone squealing resonated through the space. I scanned the darkness and in the light of the bonfire, I spotted a speaker system set some distance away from the stone circle. Chief Hayes stepped into view and cleared his throat, the microphone picking up the sound.

"I want to welcome everyone to the All Hallows Eve Bonfire. As a reminder, please drink responsibly. As is tradition here in Brookhaven, this event is meant to connect us with our community."

Ginny hurried forward with a microphone stand and the chief slid it into the holder. He made a summoning gesture and stepped aside. While his sister disappeared around the far side of the bonfire.

I watched the crowd, waiting for who would approach first. But no one did. The small clusters of people turned back to their individual conversations and food. It all felt a bit anticlimactic. Maybe everyone knew everyone else's business already. The fact that no one else went up to speak rattled my nerves and I took a step back.

"Just because no one else has gone up doesn't mean you can't be the first," Maggie urged.

"I think it's just hitting me that I'm about to reveal my magic to everyone. I had thought there would be other people before me, to sort of warm them up to the idea."

Maggie grabbed both of my hands in hers and stared into my eyes. "Darcy, you can do this. If you want them to know you the way I do, the way Tania does, then go over there and show them. And if you aren't ready, that's okay, too."

"No. I'm going to do it. I just wasn't expecting the nerves," I admitted.

Maggie leaned in and planted a kiss on my lips. I squeezed her hands and pulled her a little closer, grateful for her support. "Go show them what you're made of," she whispered as she pulled away.

Swallowing the lump in my throat, I approached the microphone stand. Sam materialized in front of me and offered a thumb's up. If I could just focus on him, maybe it wouldn't be nearly as terrifying as my mind suddenly feared it would be. I glanced at the fire behind me and shivered.

*They don't burn people at the stake anymore, Darcy,* I reminded myself.

"Uh, hello," I said, leaning into the microphone. My voice filled the open space, drawing the attention of the closest attendees. "My name is Darcy Ingram. Some of you know me. I work at High Time. I moved to Brookhaven about a year ago and while I've been here, I've discovered some things about myself. I think I'm finally ready to share my truth with everyone."

More people turned, placing their full attention on me. I could hear the shifting and rustling of fabric, and caught the glint of firelight in people's eyes as they tuned into my words. Electricity tingled at the nape of my neck as I continued.

"I am a witch. Well, a hedge witch. I came here to learn how to control this power developing inside of me and thanks to you all, I've been able to do that."

I half-expected people to demand that I provide a demonstration of my skills. Instead, no one spoke. Still they were definitely not looking away. Without thinking about it, I held my hands out. The tiny blades of grass around my feet brightened to a lush, deep green and began climbing toward the sky. I heard some people gasp as I guided the shoots, winding and twisting them into an elaborate lattice-work around me. Even though the grass was nothing more than a simple seed, I pulled delicate lily blooms and vibrant red and yellow roses out of it.

In my peripheral vision, I spotted Rick and Vinnie watching me from a distance. Vinnie's eyes had gone wide in surprise. Rick looked less annoyed than I'd expected since I was revealing my secret. In front of me, Sam slipped through the latticework and began dancing around the flames, letting out a ghostly laugh as he twirled.

I turned back toward where I'd left Maggie to see Tania standing beside her. My landlady gave me a small smile as she turned to speak to someone in the crowd. Maggie beamed and relief washed over me. I'd come out to the people who had become my community and it hadn't gone pear-shaped.

"So, uh, yeah … That's all I wanted to say. Thank you," I said.

A couple of people clapped and I thought I saw Thomas in the crowd looking awestruck. Maggie started to take a few steps my way, but stopped. I tried to go to her, but it was as if I were rooted to the spot.

The electric tingle dancing along the nape of my neck had intensified the more my magic poured into the spell. I'd never felt anything like it. Behind me the heat from the bonfire intensified, too. I pulled back on my magic, urging the grass and flowers to retreat. Before the blooms had a chance to recede though, something loud popped from behind and heat overtook me. For a split second I couldn't process what had happened. Only a louder concussive 'boom' filled my ears as the force knocked me off my feet. I slammed hard into the grasses I'd cultivated, taking the microphone stand with me. As my head collided with the ground, someone screamed and everything around me went hazy and dark.

## 4

My ears rang as the world slowly came back to me. Something hard and thin jabbed into my rib cage where I lay in the grass. Opening my eyes, the world swam around me, bringing with it a gut-roiling nausea. I quickly shut them again. Blindly, I tried to assess the rest of my body. Groping my hands along my torso, I found I'd landed on the microphone stand. Somehow I managed to roll onto my back. Nothing felt broken as I tested moving each leg and arm.

Laying there, heat washed over my face and I remembered the loud crack from behind me. What had happened? I forced my eyes open again and took in the night sky overhead, framed by the still-roaring firelight. The nausea passed more quickly this time and I pushed myself into a seated position. Sound came cascading back to me and in that moment, I wished it hadn't. The confusion of what had happened melded together in an indistinguishable cacophony of shouting voices.

"Darcy! Are you okay?" Maggie's voice cut through the muddled mess and I turned to see my girlfriend racing to my side.

"What happened?" My voice sounded miles away, which probably meant I was shouting at her.

"I'm not really sure. One minute you were making these beautiful flowers grow and then, it was like something exploded out of the fire."

"Did I do it?"

She shook her head. "I don't think so. Come on, let's get you up."

She eased me to my feet and the change in vantage point let me take stock of the rest of the people around us. No one appeared to be injured, although Vinnie and Chief Hayes were on the ground. Ginny raced to them from the other side of the fire, kneeling between them.

"Does your head hurt?" Maggie probed, tentatively touching the back of my head.

"I didn't hit my head," I answered, waving her

hand away. I turned to see Tania also laying on the ground.

Maggie must have been so focused on me that she hadn't noticed Tania's condition. I pulled free of my girlfriend's grasp and fell to my knees at our friend's side.

"Tania, can you hear me?" I shook her gently, not wanting to risk injury.

She let out a moan and opened her eyes. They were unfocused for a moment before she sat up. "I am fine." She shrugged off my attempts to help her stand.

"I think you both ought to get checked out," Maggie suggested.

Across the way, I watched as Chief Hayes and Vinnie each sat up with Ginny's help. She took each by the wrist and dragged them to where Maggie, Tania, and I stood.

"Any idea what happened?" I directed the question to Ginny.

"No idea. But that was quite the reveal you did. Don't think anyone's going to forget that for a while."

"It was so bold," Vinnie said, eyes wide.

"I just hope no one thinks I made the fire explode," I said.

"I'm taking Darcy and Tania back to the clinic for

a once over. You two should probably come, too," Maggie urged.

"But I said I am fine," Tania insisted.

"Whatever it was knocked you off your feet. You and Darcy were both unconscious for a few minutes."

"We'll go, too," Chief Hayes said.

Vinnie looked ready to protest as well, but the chief hooked a hand around the other man's elbow. He ushered him away from the festivities. I watched Ginny rush back to the microphone, scooping it off the grass and said, "Sorry for the scare. If anyone is feeling unwell, please make your way to the clinic and get checked out."

I fell into step beside Chief Hayes and Vinnie. Together we led our small procession back along Main Street to the clinic. Maggie, Ginny, and Tania brought up the rear. I was silently grateful it was just our little group that needed medical assessment.

"Has anything like that happened before?" I asked Chief Hayes as Maggie unlocked the front doors.

"No, nothing like that. Though I must admit, I wasn't expecting you to make such a huge announcement."

"It just felt like the right time."

Maggie ushered us all into the back exam area. I could see by the way her brow knit together that she wanted to check me out first, but in the fluorescent light I could see a small gash on Vinnie's forehead.

"Get him cleaned up first. I'm okay, promise."

The chief relinquished his grip on Vinnie's arm after he helped him get seated on the exam bed. I stepped out of the exam room to the small waiting area and sat in one of the plastic chairs. Chief Hayes hovered beside me while Ginny forced Tania into the second chair. With the door open, I watched as Maggie donned medical gloves and probed at the deputy's head wound. As I waited my turn for Maggie's attention, I tried to replay the scene in my head again. Hoping I could remember something that might explain what had happened.

I could recall what felt like an electrical current that intensified right before the explosion. I was fairly certain it hadn't been my magic though. For one thing, I'd never experienced anything similar. Sure, I'd connected with the residual magic in the brownie and that was not something I'd done before either. But it didn't seem logical for my abilities to take such a big leap.

"What's going on in that head of yours?" Ginny's

voice caught me off guard. I turned to see her looking at me, worry lines creasing her brow.

"Just trying to determine if I did this."

"You didn't." She sounded so definitive. "I mean ... last I checked, growing flowers doesn't make things explode."

"Do you have a theory on what happened, then?"

"Chief, you're next," Maggie interrupted, beckoning the man forward. Vinnie exited the exam room and I vacated my seat for him to take.

"No, I don't have any theories," Ginny answered, her attention drifting to Tania who was not-so-stealthily making a break for the door.

"Tania, you can't go until Maggie's given you a once over," Ginny said, pulling Tania back.

Tania glared at Ginny with a look of pure annoyance I'd never seen come over my friend before. Maybe she hit her head when she'd fallen. All the more reason for Maggie to assess her condition.

Maggie appeared and helped Tania into the exam room, casting me a worried look as she passed. Chief Hayes looked no worse for wear. "I should get back to the bonfire, reassure everyone that things are okay."

"Good idea. I'll get Vinnie home," Ginny replied.

"I can get home by myself," Vinnie said,

although his eyes went a little unfocused and glassy as he spoke.

"You might have a concussion," Maggie called. "You shouldn't be alone tonight."

Ginny exhaled. "Guess I'll take him home and stay with him, then."

"But I want to go back," Vinnie said.

"If I have to give you a direct order to go home, I will," Chief Hayes said sternly.

Somehow, that mollified Vinnie enough for Ginny to escort him off the premises. The chief followed shortly thereafter, leaving me with Maggie in the waiting area. She beckoned me into the room.

"I'll be right back. Just need to mix up something."

I stood in the doorway, studying Tania as she sat on the exam bed. I couldn't shake the feeling that something was off about her behavior, more so than just the way she'd been withdrawn since the summertime. A concussion could explain some of it. Maggie returned with a glass half full of a pale blue liquid. She handed it to Tania. "This should help you rest. I'm not seeing any signs of a concussion, but Darcy will keep an eye on you tonight. If you have anything like a headache or confusion, you need to go to the hospital."

Tania let out a prolonged sigh, but took the glass and downed the contents. I knew Maggie would want to check me over, too. Except I was worried about letting Tania leave on her own. Thankfully whatever concoction Maggie had mixed up seemed to take effect quickly and Tania settled back against the bed, eyes closed.

"Does anything hurt?" Maggie probed the nape of my neck.

"Just my ribs a little from landing on the microphone stand. But I think the grass and flowers cushioned my fall."

"It really was a beautiful display," she said, touching my side gently.

"I wasn't sure what to do to show everyone and that just came out."

"I am proud of you for sharing your truth, even if things went a little haywire after the fact."

"Did you see anything that might have caused the fire to do what it did?"

"No. I was too busy watching you." She leaned in and kissed my cheek.

"That's sweet." I leaned into her embrace. "I felt something like electricity building before it happened, on the back of my neck. You didn't notice anything like that?"

"Now that you mention it, I think I did. Like the air right before lightning strikes. But without the smell of ozone."

"What do you think it means?"

"I don't know. Honestly, this is a strange time of year around here. There's more magic in this town than any of us realize and for all we know, something reacted to your display of power."

She could be right. I had done a bit more magic than in recent months and this time, it had been out in the open. Maybe that made a difference. Still, I didn't like not having definitive answers.

"Can you come and stay at the B&B tonight?"

"Sure. Besides, it means I can monitor Tania, too."

"Thank you."

Together, we roused Tania enough to make the walk back to the B&B. I opened the front door and Maggie guided Tania upstairs to her room. That left me alone on the first floor. Despite the strange events, I wasn't ready to turn in yet. Instead, I entered the kitchen and set to making tea.

"So, that was insanity," Sam said, hovering off to my left.

"I didn't mean to cause such a ruckus."

"I don't think it was you. Well, not only you,"

Sam answered and floated toward me. "Something weird was going on before everything went boom."

"You saw something?"

"Saw? No. But I felt it building. It was like I was alive again, just for a minute. I could feel the breeze on my skin, the warmth of the fire on my face. And the smells. Oh, you have no idea how much I miss the smell of … everything."

"How is that possible?"

He shrugged, his outfit shifting from the vibrant green to a darker, more subdued blue linen dinner jacket and tight trousers. I noted a few rhinestones placed delicately on his cheek. The eyeshadow had vanished too. "I've never experienced anything like it before. And I have to admit, I wouldn't mind feeling it again."

"I felt an electrical current building before everything happened and it knocked me out. At the time I thought maybe it was the sound system acting up, but if you sensed something, then there has to be magic behind this."

"Halloween is a strange time around here."

"That's what Maggie said, too. But I didn't notice anything like it happen last year."

"All I'm saying is don't discount anything right now."

The kettle boiled on the stove. I pulled it free of the heat to fill a mug with steaming water. After a moment, I grabbed a second mug and poured the remaining water in. I added the loose tea leaves to both and waited for it to steep. Five minutes later, I carried them up to Tania's room. Maggie stood by my landlady's bedside, checking her pulse.

"Everything okay?" I leaned on the doorframe.

"Appears to be. It's all just a little weird. I mean, Tania isn't normally the type of person to ignore the possibility of injury."

"It's been a stressful couple of months. And she did hit her head. I'm sure it's nothing too serious," I answered, hoping to convince myself of her condition just as much as Maggie.

I handed over the second mug as Maggie eased the door partly shut. "I'm hesitant to leave her alone."

"What if Sam keeps an eye on her? He can let us know if something changes."

"What are you volunteering me for?" Sam's head appeared through the floorboards.

"Just hang here tonight and let us know if anything looks like it's wrong with Tania."

His jovial demeanor melted in a serious expression. "Oh, I can do that."

Maggie and I retreated to my bedroom. We sat side by side on the bed, sipping from our matching mugs. This was not at all how I expected today to go. I was grateful I'd managed to share my truth with everyone in town, even if not all of the citizens believed me. And I prayed they didn't think I had caused the explosion.

"I know you're worrying about what happened, but you didn't do anything. I think we both need some sleep," Maggie prodded as I stared at my empty mug twenty minutes later.

"You're right. I'm probably just overthinking it. Night."

I wasn't sure what woke me. Darkness filled my bedroom as I stared out at the starlit sky beyond. I was about to roll over and curl up against Maggie's shoulder when the sound of crashing and things breaking resonated through the house.

I nudged Maggie in the shoulder. "Did you hear that?"

She was slow to wake and I had to push the covers off to jolt her out of slumber. "What?" she asked sleepily.

"I heard something crash."

That got Maggie's attention and she sat up, kicking the rest of the blankets off. I scrambled for the door, ignoring the rational idea that I ought to turn on the light. Together we crept into the hallway and I stopped short of the stairs, straining my hearing in the hopes of picking up any more unfamiliar sounds.

Nothing else stood out save for what had roused me. Maybe I'd imagined the noise. I was about to tell Maggie I'd dreamt it and we should go back to bed. Only Sam's spectral form materialized in front of me. Even for a ghost, he looked spooked.

"What is it? What's wrong Sam?" I whispered, instinctively reaching for Maggie's hand.

"Tania's gone."

"Gone? What do you mean? She was asleep."

"Well she's not anymore. I don't know what she's doing, but she's definitely not acting like herself."

I thundered down the stairs and stopped at her bedroom door. It was open all the way and I could see that the bed sheets were a tangled mess at the foot of the bed. I raced down to the first floor and found shards of glass scattered on the floor. The front door was thrown wide and her car was missing.

"Why would she smash a mirror?" Maggie asked, bending down to inspect the shards on the floor.

"Maybe she didn't like what she saw?" Sam offered.

"We need to call Rick and let him know something strange is going on. Tania hasn't been acting like herself since the explosion and I don't mean just the way she's been distant. This feels like a personality change and I'm starting to get really worried about her," I confessed.

I raced back to my room and pulled my phone free from the charger. Dialing the chief's personal number that he'd provided earlier, I bypassed emergency services altogether.

Chief Hayes answered on the second ring. "Rick Hayes." To my surprise, he sounded wide awake.

"Chief, it's Darcy. I need you to get to the B&B. We have a problem ... Tania's missing."

## 5

———

The clock on the stove read just after midnight by the time Chief Hayes arrived at the B&B. I'd resisted the urge to clean up the shards of glass. If something had happened to Tania, then the mess could be evidence.

"Why don't you tell me what happened?" he inquired upon stepping into the foyer.

"We brought Tania back to the B&B from the clinic after you and Ginny left. Got her settled and we thought she'd gone to sleep. But then maybe twenty minutes ago, I woke up because I heard something. I wasn't sure what it was at first. But then I heard something break and we came down to find that the mirror was broken. Tania's car is gone too."

"Are you sure you didn't leave it behind the shops on Main?" he pointed out.

I gaped at him in embarrassment, my cheeks turning red. "Oh, I ... I forgot," I mumbled.

"Even still, Tania isn't here. We checked her room and she's gone," Maggie continued. She gestured to the mirror shards on the floor. "I don't see any evidence of blood so I don't think she cut herself."

"But how do you explain the broken mirror then if she didn't break it with her hands?" he challenged.

Maggie shook her head. "I don't have any idea. But she was acting a little off after the incident at the bonfire. Please Rick, we need to find her."

"Right, I understand your concern. I'm going to check the perimeter to make sure we aren't missing anything else like a point of entry. Why don't you give her phone a call and see if she'll answer? Maybe she just needed some air. Or maybe with everything that's happened over the past months, she went sleepwalking from stress."

With that, Chief Hayes exited through the front door. I heard him moving through the side yard. I turned to look at Maggie. "I know I haven't known Tania as long as you or Chief Hayes, but I've never seen her sleepwalk."

"Neither have I and I've known her longer than any of you," Sam interjected.

"Any thoughts on how she could have broken the mirror without touching it?" I addressed the ghost.

"I have no idea. But if you're wondering if there's something magical at play here, I would have to say yes."

"What makes you think that?" I held up a hand. "And don't tell me it's just because it's Halloween."

"You might not believe me, but this time of year, and this day specifically ... makes all sorts of things possible."

"So, what kind of magic would make Tania wander off?" I speculated aloud.

"I'm not sure, but Rick did suggest we call her. Maybe this is all a misunderstanding," Maggie said, redirecting the conversation.

"Right. Usually the simplest explanation is the right one," I said and dialed Tania's number.

It rang five times before flipping to her voicemail and I ended the call. "She didn't pick up. Are we even sure she took her phone with her when she left?"

Sam vanished, reappearing a moment later. "It's not in her room, so I'm guessing she brought it with her."

"If we go back to my place, I might be able to track her phone's signal," Maggie offered.

"I should have thought of that," I sighed. Maggie was something of an amateur hacker and her skills had come in handy more than once in the last year. Though we couldn't leave until Chief Hayes gave us the all clear.

"We need to think of all the places Tania might go," I said, leaving the foyer and entering the kitchen in search of pen and paper.

"It's the middle of the night and she's on foot. I can't imagine she'd make it too far, even in a small town," Maggie said.

"Well, uh ... there's Ginny's," I offered.

"Not that it's open right now," Maggie pointed out.

Most places in town were closed for the night, but that didn't mean Tania might not try to go there.

"Or maybe the library. I don't think they lock up," I said.

"The perimeter looks secure," Chief Hayes announced as he walked back in. "It looks like Tania took off on her own."

"We're putting together a list of places she might be able to get to on foot," I said and held up the list. "It's not much, but maybe a start?"

"We can check a couple," Maggie said.

"I'll call Vinnie back in to help search," he replied.

"Are you sure that's a good idea? It looked like he got the brunt of the explosion."

"Right. Well, then I think we ought to stick together. There's not too much trouble Tania could get up to around here, especially this late at night."

"It probably makes sense to trace her most likely route and see what we find," I suggested as Maggie and I followed the chief into the chilly autumn air. Thankfully, I'd remembered to grab my jacket and tugged it tight around my torso as the wind howled around us, sending shivers down my spine. I'd also grabbed the key and locked the front door, just to be safe.

"Does this sort of thing happen a lot around here during Halloween?" I blurted as we approached the intersection of Birch and Main Street, Ginny's café coming into view across the street. Its windows were dark.

"Some petty vandalism, silly pranks really, but nothing like people just wandering off."

"You didn't look that surprised about my big announcement," I said as we crossed the street and Maggie peered through the front window of the café.

"You told me about your abilities before, remember? And I've seen what you can do when the people you care about are threatened."

"I wasn't sure you actually believed me."

"It's a not so well-kept secret that Ginny has certain ... abilities, too. I'm more open-minded than you might think."

He had a point. For most of the time I'd lived here, our interactions had been strictly isolated to him in his professional capacity. It was clear that he took his job seriously. So, I'd assumed he was just a serious person all the time. And maybe some of his initial distrust of me had been colored by Ginny's own misgivings about my presence. From what I'd observed they were a pretty close-knit family.

"Doesn't look like she's here," Maggie called. "Let's check the library."

We moved quietly down Main Street, through the closed up tents from the festivities. We stopped at the library and then the school. However, Tania was nowhere to be found. None of this made sense.

"Should we check High Time?" Maggie suggested.

"Not sure why she'd be there, but it's worth a shot."

"Did you try her phone?" Chief Hayes interrupted.

"It went to voicemail. All we know for certain is that it wasn't in her room, so we assumed she took it with her."

"Did it go straight to voicemail or did it ring first?" he pressed.

"It rang first, which means it's on. Maybe she's somewhere she couldn't hear it?"

"It's a long shot, but what if she's at Carver's." Maggie looked at the chief and he gave a nod of understanding.

"What's Carver's?" I asked.

"A bar about a quarter of a mile up the highway."

"Could she have gotten there on foot in the middle of the night?"

"Well, depending on how much of a head start she had, it's possible."

Maggie gestured back toward the way we'd come. "Just because the car wasn't in the B&B driveway doesn't mean she didn't remember you'd parked back there. She could have gotten the car."

I took off running, leaving the other two to keep pace with me. Please let the car still be there. I didn't want to picture my friend on foot along the side of the highway. But at least that way we might be able to catch up with her. My heart dropped into my stomach as I came to a stop. The VW Bug was gone. Maggie caught up to me first and reached for my hand.

"We're going to find her," she reassured me.

"My cruiser is parked up the street. Follow me," Chief Hayes called back to us.

Maggie and I followed him and crammed into the back of the chief's police car. I shook off the unsettling feeling of riding in the back of the vehicle, separated by plexiglass. I watched as we left Brookhaven behind and turned onto the highway. The road was devoid of any other cars. The street-lights were spaced far enough apart that we dipped in and out of long stretches of shadow, setting my nerves on edge. Maggie kept a tight hold of my hand as the car turned off the highway down a short road that dead-ended at a building with a large neon sign reading Carver's in blocky letters.

"There's her car," I said, spotting the VW Bug near the front door.

Relief washed over me at the fact we'd tracked Tania down. It was short-lived as the front doors flew open of their own accord. A man came staggering through them, a bloody gash on his cheek as if he'd been punched.

Chief Hayes unlocked the rear doors and was out of the car before I'd fully registered what had happened and caught the man before he fell to the gravel. Maggie and I exited the back of the cruiser and approached the man bleeding on the ground.

"How'd you get here so fast?" another patron said, spotting the police car.

"What's going on?" I asked. Even though I realized that they owed me no explanation.

"She's crazy. He was just trying to buy her a drink and she lost it on him."

"Who?" Chief Hayes asked.

"I don't know. She just showed up ... started ranting about how she's tired of all the expectations and she just wants to live for herself for once." After a beat, he added, "She looked like she walked out of some fancy black tie thing. Big fur and everything."

"She hit me with a glass," the man on the ground added.

"That doesn't sound like Tania," I told Maggie as Chief Hayes radioed an ambulance for the man.

I knew we should wait to go in until additional law enforcement arrived, but I wasn't going to stand idly by if Tania was in danger. I let go of Maggie's hand, ran around Chief Hayes and the man on the ground, and stepped into the bar.

Dive bar didn't do this place justice. Half a dozen seats sat at the bar and not much else. A few people stood around the periphery of the room holding drinks, but most were staring transfixed at the woman sitting at the middle of the bar.

It looked like Tania. She wore the same clothes I'd last seen my landlady in when Maggie had put her to bed. But this aggressive behavior was not something I'd ever seen before.

"None of you understand how exhausting it is to feel everyone else's emotions. You just see a nice old lady and you assume, 'Oh she can handle it. It's what she's good at.' Well, no mas. I am done."

"Tania?" I said, approaching her slowly.

Only she didn't respond. I was almost afraid to touch her, but I tapped her shoulder lightly. She spun to face me. Her eyes looked as if they belonged to someone else entirely.

"You!" It came out almost like a growl. "You are a grown woman yet you act like a child ... always whining about not knowing how to control the power inside of you. Figure it out yourself."

"You don't mean that," Maggie interjected. "Come on, you've had a long night. Let's go home."

"Don't touch me. I've had enough of your help,"

Tania spat, the glass in front of her shaking as it skittered toward the edge of the bar.

I watched in confusion as the glass shot past Maggie, barely missing her by a hair before it smashed against the wall behind us. Tania raised her hands and every beverage shot into the air, eliciting stunned cries from the other patrons left empty handed. The woman might have looked like Tania, but she couldn't have been farther from the woman I knew. She let out a scream and the glasses smashed to the floor, spraying everyone and everything with stale beer and cheap liquor.

"That's it, I want her arrested and out of my bar," the bartender said just as Chief Hayes walked in.

Maggie and I backed away, careful to avoid the broken glass littering the floor. The chief approached Tania warily. I had no doubt he had misgivings about having to arrest someone he knew well. Still, he unclipped the handcuffs from his belt and held them up.

"You going to come quietly, or am I going to have to use these, Tania?"

She swiveled on the barstool to face him. She let out an exaggerated sigh and pushed off the stool. "Put your cuffs away."

Thank goodness for small mercies.

He took hold of her upper arm and guided her out of the bar. Maggie and I trailed them. An ambulance had arrived and paramedics were tending to the man she'd assaulted. He shrunk back when Tania passed and she gave him what could only be described as a wicked grin.

"I'll sit in the back with her," Maggie said when I stopped short of the police cruiser.

"Something is seriously wrong with her. Even if she got drunk, which I've never seen her do. It wouldn't make her say those things," I whispered.

"I know. We're going to figure out what happened, but first we need to get back to town."

I climbed into the front seat beside Chief Hayes while Maggie sat beside Tania in the back. Without realizing it, my right hand clenched the interior door handle in a white-knuckled grip all the way to the police station. Chief Hayes pulled the cruiser behind the building. He escorted Tania inside through the rear, ushering her into the holding cell.

"You two should go home and get some sleep. Hopefully sleeping off whatever this is will give Tania some new perspective," Chief Hayes addressed Maggie and I.

"Don't we have to give you statements about what we witnessed at the bar?" I blurted.

Chief Hayes cleared his throat. "Sorry, Vinnie usually handles that sort of thing. Give me a minute and I'll get what you need."

I gave Maggie a wide-eyed look. "Is he acting weird, too?"

She shook her head. "He's had a long night, and this isn't exactly a situation he's been in before. Let's cut him some slack."

She was probably right. I was also sleep deprived and shaken by Tania's behavior. I was probably the one not thinking straight. Chief Hayes returned with the paperwork we needed to write our statements. I wrote my statement as quickly as I could and stood outside in the chilly night air as I waited for Maggie.

As my phone's time ticked past one in the morning, Maggie appeared and wrapped her arm around my shoulders. "Come on, let's go back to the B&B. We're going to figure out what happened to Tania."

I just hoped we could fix whatever was going on. So much for a fun-filled Halloween.

**6**

___________

ania's words swirled around in my mind as I lay in bed, staring at the ceiling. "*You are a grown woman yet you act like a child ... always whining about not knowing how to control the power inside of you. Figure it out yourself!*" It sounded just as harsh replaying in my head as when she'd spoken them at the bar. Maggie snored softly beside me. I reached for my phone, the display read 3:07. We'd made it back to the B&B and decided sleep was the better course of action. Attack the problem with fresh eyes in the morning. At least, that had been the plan.

The B&B felt eerily quiet as I climbed out of bed, pocketed my phone, and padded to the door. Even when it was just Tania and I, the place still felt occupied. I couldn't quite explain it. But maybe the fact that Tania wasn't here is what made it feel empty. Pushing my unease aside, I crept into the hallway and made my way down to the kitchen. I started the coffee maker before moving to the dining room. I settled in a chair at the table and studied the empty vase at its center.

"What are you doing up?" Sam's question made me jump. Somehow, I narrowly avoided knocking the vase off the table.

"Bloody hell don't do that!" I snapped.

"Sorry. My question still stands," he retorted.

"I couldn't sleep. In case you missed it, things sort of went off the rails last night."

"Everything was going fine until that weird explosion."

"I know ... now Tania's not acting like herself. Chief Hayes had to arrest her for a bar fight," I explained, my ears perking up at the sound of the coffee pot percolating.

"Our Tania? The same sweet woman who bakes cookies and makes the most amazing empanadas?" Sam asked in an incredulous tone.

"I wouldn't have believed it either if I hadn't seen

it with my own eyes." I reentered the kitchen and plucked a mug from the rack.

"That just doesn't make sense," Sam said, bobbing up and down beside me.

"Maybe she's suffering unusual symptoms from a concussion?" I posited and took a sip from the mug. "I mean, it did look like she hit her head."

"But this sounds like a complete personality change," he pointed out.

I wanted to disagree with him, if only to quell my own fears. "She, uh, said some things that were pretty harsh to Maggie and I when we caught up to her. Plus unless she's gained some new powers lately, she's not supposed to have telekinesis."

"Well, now I know something's off," he said.

"My gut says something strange did happen to her thanks to that explosion. What do you remember?"

Sam stopped bobbing mid-air and tapped his index finger against his lips. "Well, I was pretty focused on you being all wonderful and brave—" he began.

"Right before the explosion, I felt electricity building," I interrupted.

His brow furrowed. "Now that you mention it, I

sensed something in the air. And I could swear there was some sort of presence in the fire, too.”

“Sorry, did you say *in* the fire?”

“Maybe not in it, but around it. Then it disappeared.”

“What sort of presence?”

“Honestly, I can’t say. It wasn’t anything I’d ever felt before.”

I drank more coffee, hoping it would help my muddled brain focus on what I was missing. None of this made sense. Neither Maggie nor Sam had seen anything that could explain what happened. Besides, I had my back to everything the whole time.

“Did you notice if anyone was filming me last night?” I blurted.

“Seriously. That’s a bit self-centered, don’t you think?”

If he’d been flesh and blood I would have smacked him in the arm. “I mean, what if someone caught something on video that we’re missing.”

“Oh,” he drew the word out. “Okay, that’s smart. If anyone was filming for posterity, it would have been the newspaper.”

Then that was my next stop. But not at 3:30 in the morning. I finished the coffee and my stomach gurgled as the caffeine struggled to settle in my empty stomach. I should have made tea instead to help me go to sleep again. There was no way I was making it back to bed now. Still, I tiptoed my way up to my bedroom and retrieved my laptop as quietly as I could. I made it halfway to the door before I heard weight shift in the bed.

"Darcy?" Maggie called sleepily.

"I didn't mean to wake you," I whispered. "Go back to sleep."

Maggie blinked at me through the darkness, the whites of her eyes standing out against the black. "Where are you going?"

"I couldn't sleep so I talked to Sam and he gave me an idea of where to look for some answers."

The blankets shifted as Maggie climbed out of bed. "Let me help you."

"One of us needs sleep," I noted.

"That's why they invented coffee. Come on. Fill me in on the way downstairs."

"It might be a long shot, but I'm hoping somebody was filming last night when everything exploded. Maybe we could find a different perspective."

"They might not have anything up on the newspaper feed yet. It was less than twelve hours ago," Maggie said.

She wasn't wrong. However, it was all I had to go on short of breaking into the police station and trying to reason with Tania. And obviously that wasn't going to happen. So, we settled side by side at the dining room table and I logged onto the newspaper's website.

We found a feed of photos from the first day of the Extravaganza, timestamped from early evening. But as Maggie predicted, nothing from the bonfire. I was about to navigate away from the website when Maggie jabbed her finger at the screen.

"Click there," she indicated.

I moved the cursor to hover beneath where she'd pointed to reveal a social media feed where someone had tagged the newspaper. I clicked on the link and it loaded a pair of photos depicting the moment the bonfire had erupted with the caption, 'Never a dull night in Brookhaven. Can't wait to see what Reagan from @BrookhavenTimes will make of these. #Halloween #SpooktacularSmallTowns.' In the first image, I stood weaving flowers and vines together framed by firelight. Whoever had snapped the photo had managed to catch the flowers opening into full bloom. The fire glowed behind me, swaying in the breeze. Nothing looked amiss.

"You look pretty amazing," Maggie said and I blushed.

The second showed the flames spiraling skyward in all directions, as if a glassblower was fashioning some strange piece of modern art. It had been captured mid-motion; my body flung awkwardly forward into the lattice I'd crafted. My face was blurry, but that didn't matter. I zoomed in on the background of the picture.

"Do you see that?" I turned to Maggie. "It almost looks like ..."

"Faces?" Maggie finished.

Zooming in on the image probably didn't help the quality of the photo. Though as we sat there in the early morning hours staring at it, it absolutely looked like faces were in the flames. Even for this town, that seemed beyond belief.

"Sam told me he'd sensed some sort of presence. What if he actually did?"

"I've never heard of anything like this happening."

"How much do you actually know about spirits and why some people become ghosts?"

"Not much. Sam's the only ghost I've ever met and he's not really forthcoming on details," Maggie replied.

"Yeah, he's not. But I think it's time he gets chatty."

"We don't even know if what we're seeing is really something ghost related. It could just be we're looking for an explanation and our sleep-deprived brains are seeing things that aren't really there."

"Maggie, someone else clearly thought this was strange enough to warrant posting it online for other people to weigh in."

"I just think we need to get a better sense of what this really is ... especially before we go forcing our friend to divulge information he's clearly not comfortable sharing."

"Okay. So, we should talk to Reagan. Maybe see if we can track down whoever posted these pictures."

"I'm going to head over to the station and see if Rick intends to actually keep Tania."

"If she's locked up, at least we know where she is," I pointed out.

"I'm hoping the bar incident was just a one-off thing. Besides, given the personality change, I'm worried about her having a more severe head trauma. She should be examined by a doctor," Maggie urged.

I couldn't argue with her clinical judgment. "Okay, so we divide and conquer."

We both retreated upstairs and dressed in the clothes from the day before. For a moment, I contemplated stopping long enough to make breakfast, but knew food would be available on Main Street with the Extravaganza. Maggie and I left the B&B arm-in-arm. I tried not to let worry settle too heavily over me. I just had to keep reminding myself that Tania was going to be fine and Maggie would look after her. I would figure out what happened last night and find a way to fix whatever had gone wrong.

I half-expected the street to be empty given the strangeness of yesterday evening's festivities. But there was a decent crowd even this early in the morning. I spotted a few folks browsing stalls that weren't quite open yet. I cast a quizzical look at Maggie as we neared the front door of Ginny's.

"Halloween day shopping can be even more intense than the day before," she explained.

A pang of guilt tightened my gut as I thought about Thomas manning the High Time booth solo. No, he wouldn't be alone for long, I resolved. I'd have a quick chat with Reagan and then head straight over. I wasn't going to let this interfere with my duties at High Time.

"Okay, I'll check back with you in a bit," I told Maggie as we reached the newspaper's booth.

Reagan was nowhere to be seen. Maggie gave me a quick kiss on the cheek before disappearing into the growing crowd. I stood, waiting for the proprietor's appearance.

"Can I help you?" a feminine voice asked from behind me.

I turned to see the woman who'd been operating the booth yesterday approach. She was dressed in an elaborate steampunk get-up. "Reagan, right?"

She nodded. "You're running Sage's booth, right?"

"That's me."

"The one who made the uh … memorable display at the bonfire."

"Also me," I replied less enthusiastically.

"If you're looking to run a story, that's not really how I work."

"No. Well, not exactly." I took a step closer as she moved into the booth, the table now separating us. "I'm not quite sure what happened last night. I'm pretty sure nothing I did would cause an explosion. And then I was looking at the newspaper's social media this morning and someone tagged you with some photos. And I was wondering if you might have footage from last night, too?"

"Honestly, I haven't been online this morning. I

got in late last night. What photos are you talking about?"

I pulled up the newspaper's site on my phone and toggled to the social media post with the images. She plucked the phone from my fingers, studying the image closely. "That's wild." She handed my phone back. "I'll have to check the footage we shot and see if we got anything like that."

"I've talked to a few people and they think it's just a trick of the light," I offered, hoping she'd give me her theory on what the poster had captured.

"You literally made flowers grow in mid-air last night. I'm pretty sure nothing's off-limits," she responded pointedly.

So, she believed something magical was afoot. Well, I didn't disagree. I just had to uncover its origins. "I should get going and restock our stall before things really pick up."

"I'll stop by with the footage in a bit," Reagan promised.

"Thanks."

"You know, I always sort of knew this town was different. But I never actually believed it was because of magic."

"A year ago, I wouldn't have believed it was real either."

Until Reagan gave me the footage or some other clue presented itself, all I could do was the job I was paid to handle. I darted through small knots of people to the table I shared with Thomas. The flaps were still drawn tight. A pit of dread settled in my stomach as I realized I'd failed to restock the night before.

"Oh, I'm an idiot ..." I groaned under my breath as I hastily went to untie the flaps and see how screwed we were.

"Watch your back," Thomas' voice rang out behind me. Today he'd gone for a pirate ensemble.

I spun to see him carrying fresh trays of edibles and relief washed over me in such an intense wave that my knees almost buckled. "You are a lifesaver, mate."

"Here's hoping we have as good a day as we did yesterday." He set the trays down on the table and began reorganizing them for display. "You know, I think your little chameleon buddy was our good luck charm yesterday. Any chance you could bring him back?"

I was so used to Beau appearing and disappearing on his own. Yet I'd been so caught up in the events of last night that I hadn't paid attention to where he ended up when everyone headed to the bonfire last night.

"Uh, I think yesterday was a bit much for him," I replied. "He's not used to being out and about with so many people. He's a sensitive little lad."

"I get it. Hey, I'm going to run down to Ginny's and grab a coffee. You want anything?"

"I'll take a large coffee."

I reached for my wallet, but he waved it off. "My treat."

With that, he disappeared into the crowd, leaving me to settle in behind the table. In the time it took for Thomas to return with caffeine, I'd already sold three packets of gummies and an extra-large brownie. I accepted the travel cup Thomas offered me and took a long swig.

"So, you're not even going to ask about last night?" I prompted.

"If you want to talk about it, we can. I sort of figured it was in your court."

"Maybe it's a bit selfish of me to think more people would be interested or talking about it. Even if they thought I caused the explosion ..." I cast a sideways look his way and hastily added, "Which, I didn't do by the way."

"Well, as someone who is totally normal, I

thought it was pretty cool. And I didn't think you made anything blow up."

"I appreciate the support," I said just as my phone buzzed with an incoming call from an unknown number. "Give me a second."

I stepped away from the tent and answered the call. "Hello? Who is this?"

"Darcy, it's Reagan, from the newspaper."

"Hi. Uh, how'd you get my number?"

"I ran into Maggie and she passed it along. I got in touch with our camera guy and he has some footage from last night. If you want to swing by our office now, we can go over it together."

Something about that didn't add up. I could believe that Maggie had given Reagan my number. But why would she want to go back to the newspaper's office when she was the one manning the booth for the festivities? "Um, maybe in a bit. We're just getting into the swing of sales this morning and I can't really afford to leave right now."

"I really think you're going to want to see this, though," she insisted.

I turned to see a group of what I hoped were twenty-somethings approach our tent in a tight cluster. "I really can't leave right now. I'll come by your booth around lunch."

Before she could respond, my phone beeped with an incoming call from Maggie. "Sorry, give me just a minute." I switched to the other line. "Maggie?"

"Darcy, we've got a problem."

The sense of dread I had earlier as we left the B&B returned, reminding me as it settled in my gut that I hadn't eaten anything this morning. "Is something wrong with Tania?"

"You could say that ..." she said, followed with a strained pause and then, "Darcy, she's gone. I went to talk to Rick, but he wasn't there either. And the cell door was just open and all of her belongings were missing too."

It would seem Maggie's concerns about Tania's mental state were justified. "I can't get away just now, but come to the High Time tent. We'll figure out what to do next."

Somehow, over the constant hum and chatter of voices along the street, I picked up muffled sounds on Maggie's side of the call. I thought I picked out the words "roof" and "drugs."

"Where are you right now?"

"Still by the station. I'm trying to get through, but something's going on. Hold on, let me see if—"

My pulse pounded in my neck as I waited for

Maggie to speak again. The people at our end of the street had started to turn their attention to the middle of the thoroughfare. I couldn't shake the feeling that something devastating was about to unfold.

"Oh, God. It's Vinnie!" Maggie finally said.

I didn't stop to think. I just ran. I shoved past people as they stood frozen, pointing skyward. I managed to make it to the space just outside Ginny's and looked up in time to see Vinnie standing on the roof with arms outstretched. He was laughing, head thrown back. He kept taking small shuffling steps towards the edge. I cast about, hoping to find something—anything—I could use to cushion his fall if he did indeed jump. Only there wasn't much and coaxing the tiny weeds in between the cracks in the sidewalk would take too much time.

Where was Chief Hayes?

"Don't do it," Ginny's voice rang out from high above us as she appeared on the roof with Vinnie.

"I will not be hurt," Vinnie replied. "I have been given such wonderful gifts. They will guide me safely down."

"Vinnie, you can't fly. If you jump, you're going to hurt yourself. Or worse," Ginny shouted, taking a tentative step towards him.

He looked unconvinced of her words. Given how close Ginny was to him, he believed what he told her was the truth, which raised a host of new questions. Why did he all of a sudden believe he could fly? With one last look at her, Vinnie turned back to the group congregated on the street below, gave a smirk, and launched himself into mid-air.

7

———

For a few terrifying moments, my heart stopped beating and all sound fell away. I watched in horror as Vinnie threw his body off the roof, suspended in the air high above us. I reached for Maggie's hand, unable to tear my gaze away as the rest of the onlookers stood with their focus turned skyward, too.

And then ... Vinnie flew.

It was as if a current had caught his weight like a bird and he did a lazy loop overhead, a broad grin plastered on his face. Sound came rushing back as his laughter echoed painfully in my ears. When my brain finally settled on the notion that he wasn't going to faceplant on the sidewalk, I pulled my gaze away from the antics. Turning back to the roof,

Ginny stood up there dressed in what appeared to be a handmade Sarah Sanderson costume, looking as dumbfounded as the rest of us. Our gazes met and she vanished. I assumed she was heading back to ground level.

"Okay, Vinnie, how about you come down now?" I heard Maggie call.

"Why would I do that?" he shouted back. "This is amazing!"

"You've had your fun, but it's time to get your feet back on the ground. You're scaring people."

He shook his head and went on swimming through the air as if he were doing laps in a pool. The door to Ginny's café opened and the blonde woman stepped out, approaching me.

"Did you know he could do that?" I asked, gesturing to the deputy still high above us.

"No. Then again, it seems this Halloween, lots of people are revealing things no one knew about them."

"Oh come on, it wasn't a secret to you," I noted.

"Usually, not many things are," she muttered. "Do you think you could get him down?"

"He looks pretty happy up there," I pointed out.

"But he's disrupting the event. And to be honest,

I don't know how long he's going to be able to keep that up."

As if on cue, Vinnie's body dropped a few inches in the air, eliciting several gasps from the still-assembled crowd. The wonder on Vinnie's face melted away, replaced by fear. Maybe Ginny and Maggie were right. He needed to be back on solid ground.

"I mean, I can try to get Peter Pan down, but I don't really have anything to work with."

"Would this help?" Tyson's voice caught me off guard and I turned to see him hold out a bouquet of calla lilies. He'd painted his face to look like a skeleton but he wore a tailored suit.

"I can work with that," I answered and unwound the delicate pink bow keeping the stems held together.

I laid them on the ground at my feet and turned my focus upward. The roots of my magic weren't far away and seemed to sense what was at stake. I held out my hands and my fingers began to weave, much like they'd done last night at the bonfire. The leaves on the flowers elongated and grew until they were almost vines. The flower petals stretched skyward, surrounding Vinnie's body.

"You've nearly got him," Maggie coached.

I mimed tying laces on a shoe and then lowered

my hands. I opened my eyes to find Vinnie wrapped gently inside the oversized blossoms, laying on the ground. People had given him space to land.

"Show's over," Tyson bellowed. "Everyone get back to their shopping."

The crowd dispersed and I knelt to free Vinnie from the vines and petals. "You aren't going to pull a runner are you?"

He shook his head mutely. I helped him to his feet and turned back toward Ginny. "I think we should let Chief Hayes know that Vinnie's not really fit for duty right now."

"I'll let him know," Ginny answered, hooking her arm through Vinnie's. "Come on. You're coming with me."

Before I could say anything more, the pair of them disappeared into the crowd in the direction of Ginny's booth. My fingers were still entwined in the vines and petals of Tyson's flowers. I'd never tried to work something back into its original shape before my magic took over. Though I realized, I had no idea what Tyson had intended for the flowers. It would be rather rude of me to accept them to help Vinnie get grounded and then not return them. So, with concentration I coaxed them back to normal size. I scooped up the discarded ribbon and hastily tied it back around the stems. "Thanks for these," I said, handing the pawn shop owner the reassembled bouquet.

"Happy to help. But something strange is definitely going on. Even for this town."

"Any theories?" I prodded with a hopeful lilt to my voice.

"I don't like to speculate, but last night I swear I saw something come out of the bonfire."

"What sort of something?"

"I don't know exactly. It was a blink and you'd miss it sort of thing. But it could have been a trick of the light. Maybe I'm just looking for explanations where there aren't any to be had."

"I don't think you were seeing things," I said.

Just then, Maggie caught my attention, gesturing toward a less populated area of Main Street. Tyson spotted her, too, and made a shooing gesture.

"See you around, Darcy."

I joined Maggie and exhaled. "We aren't the only ones who think something strange happened last night. Tyson says he thought he saw something come out of the fire."

"Did he have any idea what sort of thing?"

I shook my head. "Before you called, Reagan called me to say she had video footage from last night. She wanted to meet at the newspaper office. It seemed kind of strange given the Extravaganza is happening out here."

Maggie shrugged. "Maybe she just has a better connection there? I mean, video files can be big and lag if they're on an unsecured connection."

"Maybe. But she also insisted I meet her immediately."

"Well, then maybe we shouldn't keep her waiting," Maggie suggested.

"I guess it's worth checking out. But I need to make sure Thomas can handle the booth."

"I'll meet you back here in ten minutes," Maggie said. "I'm going to see if I can find anything that might give us a hint at where Tania went."

As I retraced my steps back to High Time's booth, I scanned the crowd, hoping Tania had come to her senses and was browsing the handmade wares on display. None of the brunettes I passed turned out to be my landlady.

"Hey, you're back," Thomas greeted. "I heard someone say Vinnie jumped off a building. That's nuts."

"Yeah, there's a lot of weird things going on around here lately. Look, I hate to bail on you, but I'm worried about Tania. She's missing and acting oddly since last night. Maggie and I are going to look for her."

"Hey, do what you need to. I can hold down the fort here," he said.

"You're the best. I owe you."

"What are co-workers for?" he replied with a grin.

With the booth in good hands, I went to rejoin Maggie. The excitement over Vinnie's impromptu flight had died down and the crowd had settled back into a more organized chaos. Even though it was barely ten in the morning, I spotted small clusters of children already in their costumes ready for trick-or-treating. I spotted more than a couple of witches with their puffy skirts and conical hats secured below their chins with thin straps. They waved as they ran by, chasing each other and squealing with delight.

"Any luck finding Tania?" I asked when I found Maggie.

"No. I've been trying Rick, too, but his phone keeps going straight to voicemail."

"Even when you call the station?"

She nodded. Okay, that didn't bode well. With Vinnie out of commission, Chief Hayes was our only law enforcement officer. But surely Ginny had filled him in on the situation with Vinnie. Maybe he was off looking for Tania on his own and had forgotten to charge his phone.

"Well, let's not panic yet," I said, trying to convince myself as much as my girlfriend that things weren't about to go off the rails completely.

"You know, why don't we swing by the newspaper's booth and see if Reagan is still there? For all we know, she went to the office and then when you didn't show up, she went back to selling subscriptions and her hand-decorated tote bags."

"Yeah. That would make sense."

I tried to enjoy the camaraderie of the townspeople as they celebrated Halloween, but the cloud of unease that followed our every step made it hard to appreciate my community. Maggie's hand slid into mine and I focused on the feeling of her fingers laced through my own, and the steady pressure of her arm against me as we walked.

My heart dropped into my stomach as we approached the booth and Reagan was nowhere to be seen. I forced myself to take a few deep breaths and could sense Maggie trying to keep me calm.

"Let's head to the office, then," she suggested, not giving me the chance to vocalize my panic.

She tugged me along the street that ran parallel

to Main and behind the shops where everyone had parked their cars. It felt a little illicit to sneak in through the rear, but we didn't want to draw a lot of attention our way. The back door to the newspaper's offices sat ajar and unlocked , propped open by a loose brick.

"That looks suspicious," I noted, moving it to create a wider opening.

"It is kind of odd, but I'm trying not to find conspiracies where there aren't any," Maggie answered. "Besides, honey, not to sound judgmental, but you've barely slept. You're a little extra jumpy."

I couldn't dispute her words. I was running on not enough sleep and caffeine. I'd definitely neglected breakfast this morning, too. I needed to remedy at least one of those things soon. But at the moment, I wasn't sure which trumped the others.

"Reagan, are you in here?" I called as we walked into the main area of the office.

The lights overhead were off and didn't come on with our entrance. Maggie left my side in search of a switch. A moment later, the bulbs turned on overhead, revealing the space was uninhabited. A couple of desks took up some of the space with large monitors on each. I spotted a pair of high-end printers along the far wall. A lone laptop sat open on one of the desks as well.

"You still not finding this really suspect?" I questioned as I pointed to the computer.

"Yeah, okay now my conspiracy radar is pinging," Maggie agreed. "Maybe we should leave?"

The rational part of me agreed with her suggestion. We didn't have a real reason to be here. I was beginning to question whether Reagan had actually called me at all. That posed a whole new question, could someone possess the ability to mimic other people's voices? The thought sent shivers down my spine. The curious part of my nature, however, wanted to know what was on the laptop. Maybe whoever had called really did have bonfire footage. And without more, we were simply spinning our wheels, which didn't get us any closer to figuring out how to help Tania and Vinnie.

"Someone wanted me to see what's on this computer. Whether it was Reagan or someone else, we're here. My gut tells me it has information that we need to help our friends."

"Okay. I should have known not to argue with you when you're on a case," Maggie said with a smile.

"Are you saying I'm difficult?"

"No, of course not. You just get this sort of intensity when you're working through a problem, especially one that threatens your friends. I admire that about you. I know if I'm ever in trouble, you won't stop until you've solved the case."

"I swear I never thought this would be who I am ... an amateur sleuth. But Ginny was right when she told me I was suited for it."

"Well, come on then Miss Sleuth, let's see what we came here for."

I stepped up to the desk and ran my finger over the trackpad to wake up the computer. In that instant, I realized we might have come for nothing if we couldn't access the machine. Maggie might be good at cracking tech puzzles, but even she probably couldn't hack the login.

Except the laptop was unlocked and when the screen turned on, it queued up a video with a big triangle 'Play' button in the center. Definitely a little too convenient. I could see the time and date stamp in the upper left corner confirming it was taken last night.

"Here goes nothing," I muttered and hit 'Play.'

Maggie and I leaned in as the video played. Reagan appeared on the monitor, microphone held just below her chin.

"Hey there, Brookhaven. While I'm sure many of you are here tonight with us, I always make a point to record big events for those members of our community who aren't able to join us in person. We've brought back the bonfire this year and it's shaping up to be just as memorable as in years past." Behind her, I spotted myself stepping up to the microphone stand. "It looks like we've got our first person to share."

I hit fast-forward on the video. I already knew what I'd said. I didn't need to hear it again. Although, a part of me was curious to see reactions from the crowd. Still, if things didn't get any weirder, Reagan would post this online and I could watch it to my heart's content on repeat later.

"Stop there," Maggie said.

I hit 'Play' again and watched as I wove grasses and flowers together in a latticework. I'd been the one to do it and yet I found myself almost mesmerized by the process.

"There's definitely something there," Maggie said, pulling my attention away from the magic.

I cleared my throat and rewound the video a few seconds. I tried to focus on the surrounding area. Behind me, the fire crackles and spits embers skyward. Nothing unusual about that. I could see

Chief Hayes and Vinnie standing on the left of the screen and just barely made out Tania on the right. The camera moved to the side and I lost my view of Tania as well as the chief and Vinnie. Something blinding and white flashed across the screen just a few moments before the fire exploded.

"What was that?" I blinked, trying to clear my vision.

"I don't know. But look at that." Maggie directed my attention back to the video.

I studied the screen again as the video turned away from the flames erupting outward. In the darkness I could make out those same faces that the social media poster had spotted in their stills. And just before the video cut out, I could swear I saw gauzy figures emerge from the flames before speeding away into the night.

## 8

I couldn't have seen what I thought I saw. I rewound the video and played it again, looking feverishly for a way to slow the footage down. I bent until my face was mere centimeters from the screen, watching the brilliant flash of light and then the figures emerged. I hit pause before they vanished, trying to track the trajectory.

"What are you seeing?" Maggie prompted.

I held up a finger to signal I wasn't ready to answer her question yet. I hit 'Play' again and in my mind's eye I oriented myself to where Tania, Vinnie and Rick had been standing. The figures faded away at the edges of the camera's range. I could almost make out the pattern on Tania's sleeve before the image went dark.

"They disappeared," I finally answered.

"But you saw something else," Maggie noted.

"If I didn't know things like magic and ghosts were real, I'd say it was a trick of the light. But, I do know those things actually exist, and I think, maybe they disappeared *into* other people."

"So, you think Tania and Vinnie are ... possessed?"

"Ginny said she'd never known Vinnie to possess magic and he was definitely using it when he jumped off the roof. It would explain Tania's sudden magic change."

"Is that even possible?"

I only knew one person we could ask. "We need to talk to Sam."

"When in need of ghost info, go to the source. Smart."

I still didn't like that we'd been led here. It felt like a set up and the fact that Reagan never appeared worried me. I didn't know her well, but she hadn't struck me as the type to set me up or lead me into a potentially dangerous situation.

"Is there anything more you think you could get off the video?" I turned to my girlfriend.

"I doubt it. The camera angle isn't great. Even if I was able to slow it down, which is what I'm guessing you're getting at, it was so dark and weirdly lit that it would just pixelate."

It was worth a try. Maybe we'd have more luck with Sam back at the B&B. We left the newspaper office the same way we came in. Maggie was sure to turn off the lights and set the laptop to sleep mode to hide our entry. Still I didn't allow myself to exhale until we were back on the street surrounded by Brookhaven's residents.

"We're going to figure this out," Maggie told me as we wove our way through the crowd on the street.

I spotted Reagan back at her booth and veered that direction. She looked surprised when our gazes met.

"Why didn't you show up at the office?" I demanded, not bothering with pleasantries.

"I know I said it was urgent, but then Vinnie jumped off the roof," she explained.

"Did you leave the footage for me to find?"

Her brow knit together. "No. I didn't." She turned to a stocky bloke with two inch gauge earrings in both ears. "Steve, did you take that footage from last night back to the office?"

"Yeah. You asked me to. Said you needed to show it to someone. So I queued it up."

Relief hit me in a powerful wave. We hadn't been

set up after all. Reagan had in fact called me and her staff had set up the footage.

"Sorry for being a bit aggressive just now," I apologized to Reagan.

"It's fine. Did you find what you were looking for?"

"I'm not sure exactly. But I think it gave me a place to look."

"Good luck."

I linked my arm through Maggie's and we pivoted, heading back down the street towards Tania's. I sucked in a deep breath as we reached the front porch of the B&B. Nothing looked amiss and yet I couldn't shake this odd energy that came over me as we entered.

"Sam? I need to talk to you," I called from the foyer.

No answer.

*'Tania's room.'*

Beau's voice resounded in my head. Even after spending a year with the telepathic reptile, he still made me jump from time to time. I turned toward the bannister. Sure enough, the wood rippled at the very edge to reveal Beau curled up, his tail looping around the banister itself.

"Thanks," I said and gave the chameleon a quick pet along his back.

I led the way upstairs to Tania's room. Beau's words had only given us a location, not any context for what we might find. Had Tania returned home after her jailbreak? Or was Sam posted up waiting for her return? The door was open and I couldn't make out the sounds of anyone rummaging through things. That suggested whoever was inside was incorporeal.

"Sam, you in here?" I called before entering.

Sam hovered by the window, staring out at the backyard. He didn't even turn when I called his name. That was troubling. Maggie made a little gesture to signal I should approach him solo. So, I walked around the foot of the bed to stand at the window.

"You okay, mate?"

"Something is wrong with Tania," he said. "Seriously wrong."

"We know. Or at least we're beginning to piece together a theory. It's actually why we came to the B&B. We need to pick your brain."

The repeated use of the word 'we' piqued his curiosity enough for him to do a little half spin to see Maggie standing behind him. "What's your theory?"

"We saw some raw footage from the bonfire last night," I began.

"How? Where? When?" Sam peppered me with one-word questions.

"That's not important. The contents of the video are what has us wondering about ... well ghosts."

"What about ghosts?" I immediately picked up on the defensive tone in his voice, especially the last word.

"Well, you're the only one I've ever met."

"I am unique," he said with a little twirl, and a bit of his sassy persona coming through his otherwise morose appearance.

"We know you are, but you can't be the only ghost to ever have existed," Maggie pointed.

"For one thing, ghost stories would be far more fabulous," I added.

"Look, if this is some way to butter me up to talk about my ... experience, it's something very personal and I don't want to get into it," Sam answered.

I couldn't deny I was curious about his story, but I respected his privacy. When he was ready to share, he would. "No, nothing like that. Just, what sort of circumstances would lead to someone becoming a ghost?"

"Traumatic deaths are usually the most common," Sam said slowly. "Though, I think sometimes people linger, because they had such a deep connection to the living that the universe doesn't want to sever that link."

"Can ghosts be summoned? Like, with a séance or something?"

"No. Ghosts are already tethered to this plane. They can't be summoned from anywhere else."

"Are you sure?"

"In my experience, no one would be able to summon me."

"It's just, what we saw in that video suggests ... " I trailed off.

"It looked like something came out of the fire last night and disappeared into the night. Or maybe into people?" Maggie finished for me.

"And you said you felt a strange presence," I added.

"But that wouldn't be ghosts."Sam turned fully from the window. "What you're describing, that sounds more like spirits. And before you ask, yes there's a difference."

"Please, enlighten us," I urged.

"Spirits are incorporeal much like your normal

ghost. But they're the soul of a dearly departed person who had the luxury to move on after death. They haven't been around for a while. And while I can't confirm this for a fact, I've heard that they tend to be supernaturally gifted in life."

"So what, we're thinking someone has summoned some magical spirits and they're now possessing Tania and Vinnie?" Maggie asked.

"Is that something a spirit could do?" I looked at Sam for confirmation.

"Maybe. That bit's a little iffy, too. I would guess it depends on who was summoning them and for what purpose," Sam explained. "You'd need to talk to an actual witch about that sort of thing."

"Hang on a minute, you said they're usually supernatural when they're alive. Does that mean ghosts are normal folks?" I posed.

"I mean, most of us, yeah. I guess if a witch or something died a horrific death, you might end up with something like a poltergeist," Sam mused.

My mind wanted to sit and analyze, then synthesize all of this information. But we still didn't know where Tania had gone or what antics Vinnie might pull next. And I had to believe that the fact today was Halloween couldn't be a coincidence. Sam had said the veil between the living and the dead frayed on days like today. It stood to reason that the change would have started the night before.

"So, hypothetically, if someone did summon some spirits and they did manage to possess people, what would that do?"

"I may be a ghost, but I'm not omnipotent. Since my death, I've never left Brookhaven. Sure, there's supernatural types here, but most of them don't bother me, so I don't bother them. What I'm saying is, I'm not an expert."

"Then we need to find someone who would know about this kind of thing," I proclaimed.

"There aren't exactly many out and proud witches in this town. You and I make up like half of them," Maggie reminded me.

We weren't likely to get Tania to talk, even if we could find her and Ginny was busy wrangling Vinnie. "It's a long shot but I might know someone who could help."

Maggie fixed me with a quizzical look as I pulled out my phone and dialed one of my contacts. Setting the call on speaker, I listened as it rang twice.

"Darcy, love? Is everything okay?" Nan answered.

"Hi Nan, actually no. Things are a bit bonkers

right now and I was hoping you might be able to give me some advice?"

"I can try. What's going on?"

"Well, I'm here with my girlfriend Maggie," I began. "Anyway, last night, we think someone might have summoned some spirits. Not ghosts, there's a difference apparently. Those spirits might be possessing two of our friends. But we don't know much about summoning spirits."

The line was quiet for a moment before Nan said, "I went to a few séances in my youth but to be honest, I never really believed we were communing with the dead. Not then, anyway. I did meet a woman a few years back who I could sense had that sort of ability; to commune with those long past living. She told me about a book of spells she used." Feedback filled the connection as Nan moved around. "She gave me a copy; not that I've ever had a reason to use it. Let me see if I can find it and I'll send you the information."

"From the times you did séances, did they ever say anything about what might happen once someone was possessed?" Maggie chimed in.

"They never lasted more than a few minutes. Why, how long has it been since you suspect your friends have been taken over?"

I checked the time. "Over twelve hours. They've been acting really not themselves. Someone who doesn't have any magical ability was able to fly in mid-air off a roof."

"Hmmm, now that's interesting. Magic is in the blood. Even if someone was possessed, it shouldn't give mundane people special abilities."

I looked at Maggie. "Is it possible Vinnie actually has magic and he just never knew? I mean, I didn't come into my power until my thirties."

"I feel like right now anything's possible," Maggie said.

"Do you have any idea where this might have happened?" Nan interjected.

"Yeah, at a bonfire last night. Pretty much everyone in town was present. Why?"

"There were always bits and bobs at the séances to represent the person we were trying to contact. If someone purposely cast a spell to summon the dead, they'd need something to connect to, a way to anchor them here."

"I didn't see anything like that last night. But I was more focused on other things," I admitted.

"Me, too," Maggie agreed. "But with what happened and the event today, I bet things haven't been completely cleaned up yet. We could head over and look around."

"I'm sure Tyson wouldn't mind if we offered to clean up," I said.

"Be aware, you want to be careful with whatever you find. From my experience, only the person who summoned a spirit can send them back into the realm of the dead," Nan said.

"Thanks Nan. I promise, we'll be careful."

I ended the call and pocketed my phone. "I guess we're off to go spirit hunting."

"What about Tania?" Sam hovered in front of me, as if he could actually bar my path forward.

"Until we know who cast this spell, we can't help her. But we do need to know where she's gone. Could you try to find her?"

"I'll do my best. But I can't go beyond town limits."

We would have to hope Tania had stayed in town this time. We made it down to the first floor when I realized that Beau had no idea what was going on. He still lounged on the bannister and looked up at me when I ran the tip of my index finger along his back.

"I'm not sure how much you know about what's going on Beau," I said softly.

Beau blinked at me once. *'Tania, not herself.'*

"Yeah. We're trying to fix it. Is there any way you'd be able to help Sam track her down?"

*'No.'*

It was worth a try. "You might still be able to help us. Come on."

I extended my arm and he detached from the wood, climbing up to perch on my shoulder like a parrot. I felt a ripple of energy as he made himself invisible.

"Darcy, have you thought about what happens when we find out who cast this spell?" Maggie broached as we headed toward the edge of town and Tyson's property.

I stopped mid-step to consider her words. "Whoever did this had a reason for it. Once we know who's behind it, we'll find a way to stop them."

"I just hope Tania and Vinnie don't remember what they've done," Maggie muttered as the backside of Tyson's shop came into view.

I hoped so, too. I had to believe most of what Tania had said came from whoever was using her body. My friend would never be so callous and mean. The remnants of the bonfire weren't hard to find and neither was Tyson. He stooped in the grass, picking up shards of wood splinters.

"Want a hand?" I called.

He stood and pivoted to look at me. He'd cleaned off the face paint from earlier. "Don't you have a booth to run?"

"Something's happened to Tania and we're trying to figure out how to help her. We think whatever it was, happened here," I said as vaguely as possible.

"I take it that whatever is going on with her is the same thing that's affecting Vinnie and the Chief?"

I blinked at him. "Chief Hayes was fine."

Tyson shook his head. "I just saw him about five minutes ago before he took off into the woods and uh, he wasn't wearing any clothes."

That *definitely* didn't sound like the Rick Hayes I knew. "Yes, whatever we find we're hoping it helps all of them."

He gestured around the space. "Have at it, then, ladies."

I stepped over the remnants of the vines and flowers I'd created the night before and started to circle the bonfire. Most of the support structure was still intact, obscuring my view. I circled it and stopped on the opposite side, spotting something silver glinting in the morning sun. Gingerly, I picked it up to find part of a bracelet that looked antique. Good thing we had someone skilled in judging objects' provenance on hand to tell us what we might be looking at.

"Look at this," Maggie said, holding up a burned bit of paper with cramped handwriting on it.

I could make out the word 'spell.' We were definitely on the right track.

## 9

I reached for the bracelet bare-handed when I felt a tiny claw dig into my shoulder.

'*Dangerous. Use protection.*'

I hadn't thought about it, but if the bit of jewelry had somehow been used in summoning spirits, there could be residual magic.

"Maggie, do you have anything I could use to pick this up without letting it touch my skin?"

My girlfriend produced a pair of latex medical gloves from a pocket. She tossed them over from where she stood on the left hand side of the pyre. I donned the gloves before I pocketed the jewelry and turned my attention back to searching. A few other bits of paper hadn't been consumed by the fire and I scooped them up. I doubted we'd be lucky enough to piece together the whole paper, but maybe we'd recover something to give us a hint as to who was behind it.

"There's another bit of jewelry over there," Maggie said, gesturing to the far side of the pyre.

I crouched down, brushing dirt and dust away to reveal a simple cross on a chain along with a ring. I retrieved them and straightened up. Tyson continued gathering trash and debris a short distance away in the field.

"Hey, Tyson, could you look at something for us?" I called.

He turned at the sound of my voice, set down the bag he'd been using for rubbish collection, and closed the distance between us.

"Would you by chance know how old these are? Or if they're real silver?"

"Meet me in my shop. I'll take a look."

I felt pressure on my shoulder again and held out my arm for Beau to climb down so I could look at him. "We're going to be careful," I told him, hoping to preempt his warning.

*'Sam needs help.'*

"We can't go right now," I answered.

*'I go. Home.'*

"Okay. Stay safe."

Hopefully, we wouldn't need his camouflaging abilities anytime soon. I watched as he vanished again from sight.

"I wish I knew how he did that," Maggie said.

"Me too." It was a mystery for another day.

Maggie led the way around the exterior of the pawnshop to the front door. She tried the handle to find it locked. A moment later I heard the metallic click of the locking mechanism disengaging and Tyson pulled the front door open. The space felt less cramped for some reason even though all three of us stood on the patron side of the counter. The lighting was brighter, too. Maybe the air of mystery had simply been dispelled.

"Put them on the counter," Tyson instructed as he moved through the partition in the counter to stand opposite Maggie and I.

I laid the pieces on the bit of velvet he'd spread onto the wooden countertop. He studied them each in turn.

"Their style suggests they're several hundred years old. The way the chain is secured and the cross is soldered to the chain instead of strung," he explained.

"The ring looks similar to what one might have

seen women receive as wedding bands. This one is rather simple, a braided design with something like a thin vein of gold in it. It would have belonged to someone with status."

"What about the bracelet?"

"It's been damaged. But it looks to be from the same time period." He turned over the bracelet and moved a lighted magnifying glass over to better view the jewelry. "It looks like there is some sort of inscription or monogram on the inside."

I leaned in closer to the magnifying glass to see if I could spot what he'd noticed. I could make out something like indentations in the metal, but what they said was beyond me. Tyson leaned back, lips pressed into a thin, determined line. Without a word, he left the front of the shop, taking the bracelet with him. I turned to Maggie, offering a confused look.

She shrugged. "I didn't see anything, but I also don't stare at precious objects for a living. If he sees something that might give us a clue to who this belonged to and who might be inhabiting our friends, then I think we need to be as patient as possible."

I didn't disagree with her sentiment. Though the longer we stood here in the shop without answers, the more I couldn't shake this impending sense of unease. I couldn't explain why I felt this foreboding, and yet it was definitely there. After what felt like ages, Tyson returned, holding up the bracelet for our inspection. The tarnished metal was now glistening and bright from being cleaned. He laid the object back under the lighted magnifying glass and I could clearly make out the initials C.H. etched into the underside of the metal.

"Give me a minute to inspect the other items again to see if they're part of a set," Tyson said, snatching up the necklace and ring.

He left Maggie and I alone again. This time, though, he returned in under a minute, a look of excitement in his eyes. I'd never seen the man look so giddy over items in his shop. "They aren't a set. And yet, I get the sense they are still part of a collection."

He turned the ring to reveal a tiny P.H. and the necklace revealed an A.H. He was definitely right, the jewelry all appeared to have some sort of connection. A thought nagged at the back of my mind as I studied the objects. It stayed at the very outer recesses of my memory, refusing to come into the light of day.

*What am I not remembering?*

"Tyson, you said they could be from the 1700s?" Maggie probed, claiming my attention.

"Best guess, yes." he noted and cocked his head to one side. "What are you thinking?"

"We aren't the first witches to pass through this town," Maggie answered, looking slightly surprised by her own admission.

Tyson's shop had a truth charm placed on it, so that anyone who came in could only tell the truth about the items they brought for his appraisal and purchase. I'd never gotten the full story, but someone had burned Tyson in the past. Now he was assured to protect his business.

I let Maggie's statement roll around in my head for a moment. Something about witches and Brookhaven. What was it?

"Oh, bloody hell!," I blurted as the realization came over me like a ton of bricks knocking me off balance. "You're right. Witches were in this town, and they went all the way back to the 1700s. Earlier even."

"Yeah, but you don't really think ... " Maggie began.

"That Ginny could have had something to do with it?" I finished for her thanks to the spell compelling the truth.

*A spell that Ginny had given Tyson.*

"Her family does date back to the Witch Trials in this area," Tyson confirmed.

That was what my memory had been trying to tell me. I didn't doubt Ginny could be powerful enough to pull off summoning spirits. But why would she want to and let them possess people close to her made little sense. We were missing something here. And it would only be revealed by going to the source.

"You've been really helpful, Tyson. Thank you," I said and gestured to the jewelry. "Do you mind if we take this with us?"

"It's not yours to sell. I'll give it over only if you promise to get it back to the rightful owner."

"We will," I answered.

He produced a small velvet pouch and slid the ring, necklace, and bracelet into it before passing it over the counter. I pocketed the bag and turned to Maggie. "We need to find Sam and see if he's tracked down Tania."

"What about Ginny?"

My instincts told me she'd be out on Main Street selling coffee to the townsfolk all day. After all that's what was expected of her and she was deeply invested in keeping Brookhaven's traditions alive. Besides, I doubted she'd turn down a profit.

"We'll find her after. I don't think she's going anywhere."

MY MIND SPUN TRYING to piece together details I didn't have yet. How had Ginny managed it? And did these items really belong to her long-dead ancestors? Why had she done it? Part of me wanted to go up to her and ask point blank, but I couldn't go accusing her of something, not when she was the town's resident Queen Bee. We'd become something akin to friends in the last few months and I wasn't going to jeopardize our relationship without having more information. As Maggie and I moved down the street, I realized I didn't have a way to actually get in touch with Sam. I'd just have to trust that he would find me.

We reached what used to be Beekman Family Butchery and stopped. I still couldn't walk past it without getting a touch nauseated. The owner had conspired with a local vampire and had harvested the organs of the vampire's victims to sell on the black market. He'd also been partly responsible for

Tania's abduction and imprisonment by the same said vampire. As I stared at the empty shop window, I felt my phone buzz with an incoming message. I fished it out of my pocket to find Nan had sent an email. She'd taken a photo of the front cover of the spell book she referenced on our call. An accompanying message also noted that I could possibly find it in digital format. I couldn't help but chuckle to myself at the thought of how modern witchcraft had become.

"Maybe we could figure out what spell Ginny used and reverse engineer a solution," I said.

"Or we should just ask her to her face. If this is her doing, she needs to explain herself."

"Oh good, there you are," Sam's voice interrupted the flow of the conversation. He materialized in front of me. "So, it's a good news, bad news sort of thing."

"Start with the good news. I could use some of that right about now." I held my phone up to my ear to ensure no one else would think I was talking to thin air. Magic was real and people might believe in witches, but there were still limits.

"Well, I found Tania. And she didn't leave town."

That was good news. "Okay. What's the bad news?"

"Well, she spotted me and let's just say the words that came out of her mouth were not ones I'd ever expect to hear from Tania Alvarez."

"That was our experience, too. It's like she's got all this pent up anger inside of her and she's just letting it out," Maggie interjected.

"I think your theory that she's been possessed by a spirit is spot on. She had this sort of weird aura around her."

"Do you think maybe the person we've been talking to is actually this spirit and not Tania?" I suggested.

"Maybe?" Sam shrugged his translucent shoulder. "The way she spoke ... it didn't sound like Tania. But the things she talked about were things only Tania would know. So, maybe it's a mix of both?"

"Unfortunately, it's not just Tania we're worried about now," I said, patting the pouch with the jewelry in my pocket. "Vinnie and the chief are both affected, too."

"That explains why no one's showed up to arrest her," Sam muttered.

"Sam, Beau left because he sensed you needed help," I pointed out.

"I thought I saw him for a second while she was

hurling insults, but then he vanished again. My guess is he went back to the B&B," Sam answered.

"Where is Tania now? Is she going to get herself or anyone else hurt?" I tried not to let panic seep into my tone.

"Oddly enough, she's at church. Broke a couple of statues. So some minor vandalism. I'm sure she'll feel really bad about it once she's, uh, you know, not possessed anymore."

"Keep tabs on her. We think we've got an idea of who might be behind this," I said.

"As you may have noticed, I did not die with a cell phone attached to my person. I can't exactly keep an eye on her while I come looking for you."

"Can you and Beau communicate?"

"Me and that little guy are thick as thieves. If he calls out, I would hear him."

I guess I shouldn't have let Beau leave while we were with Tyson. I turned to Maggie. "Do you think you can swing by the B&B and pick him up again?"

"Sure. What are you going to do?"

"I think things may go a little smoother if only one of us brings up the whole 'I think you raised spirits that hijacked my friend' topic."

"Okay, that's fair. I'll meet you at Ginny's booth in ten minutes."

I gave her a quizzical look "From here, the B&B is less than five minutes away and I'm pretty sure Beau isn't going to need much convincing to come along to help Tania."

"No. But there's one other thing I want to do beforehand. Trust me, I think it's going to help." She gave me a swift kiss on the lips before hurrying away from the old butcher shop and then disappeared through a break in the line of booths.

That left me standing alone as I tried to drum up the courage to approach one of the most powerful witches in Brookhaven. I took a deep, centering breath and marched down the row of booths until I came to the one selling her signature blend of coffee. Vinnie sat in the seat behind the table looking miserable.

"You doing okay, Vinnie?" My question caught him off guard and he looked at me with a startled expression. I noted a bright pink flower tucked behind his ear and he'd donned a vibrant yellow shawl over his deputy's uniform.

"That woman will not release me. She has chained me here like some common animal. I simply wish to be free." His eyes lit up. "Can you release me?"

He didn't sound like Vinnie at all. "What woman?"

He shook his head. "I do not recall her name." He craned his neck to look past me and jutted his chin out. "There, that one. The woman with the bright yellow hair."

I turned to see Ginny approaching, carrying a to-go cup with her shop's logo on it. I turned back to Vinnie and realized what he meant by 'chained.' Ginny had handcuffed one of his wrists to the support beams of the booth. He wasn't going anywhere unless the tent went with him. And he hadn't really reacted when I'd called his name. Rather, it was as if he didn't recognize his own name.

"This is going to sound like a silly question, but I want you to answer me honestly," I said and he turned all of his focus back to me. "Can you tell me your name?"

"Agatha Hayes."

*A.H.*

That was more confirmation that Ginny was at the very least connected to what was going on. The way Agatha spoke suggested she came from a simpler time. One without modern conveniences and probably less openly practiced magic. Was it her magic on display when Vinnie leapt off the roof earlier? Was it even possible for her to transfer her powers to him?

"Here, drink this. It will help your head," Ginny said, thrusting a cup into Vinnie's unsecured hand. It took her a moment to register my presence. "Shouldn't you be selling pot brownies down the street?"

"Thomas has it covered. Actually, I need to talk to you," I said, closing the already short distance between us.

"About what?"

"How about why you summoned a bunch of spirits who are now possessing our friends?"

Ginny's cheeks paled to an almost deathly pallor and a second cup trembled in her hands. Her whole body shook as she processed my statement. "Not here. Meet me behind the café in five minutes. I'll explain everything."

**10**

───────

didn't like the idea of leaving Vinnie—or Agatha—alone and handcuffed to a tent. Still, everyone else didn't seem to notice the oddity. And for the moment, he looked content to sip from the cup Ginny had given to him. I started heading toward the back of the row of shops and spotted Maggie approaching me with something tucked under her right arm. I didn't see Beau, but that didn't mean he wasn't present. This many people tended to make him shy. Plus, he'd been very active the day before. I was beginning to understand just how much those who possessed powers on the emotion side of things needed more time to recover from using their powers.

I hurried to meet my girlfriend and gestured to a

side street that would take us around behind the shops. "Ginny wants to talk to me."

"Should I hang back here then?"

I bit my lip, trying to decide on the best course of action. On the one hand, I still didn't want to gang up on Ginny. On the other, it would be far easier to come up with a game plan if Maggie was present, too. Besides, I doubted if Ginny would be at all surprised to see Maggie join us. "Come with me."

She handed me the tablet as we walked and gestured for me to tap the screen. I did so and found the same book cover that Nan had sent me, filling up the available space. I gave the screen a tentative swipe to the left and found that it moved to the book's Table of Contents. I understood now what she needed the extra time for. We turned the corner at the end of the side street and I spotted Ginny standing at the back door to her café. Her white blonde hair stood as a stark contrast against the brickwork behind her. Her head swiveled at the sound of our approach and her shoulders, which had been up near her ears, relaxed a little. Hmm, that was surprising.

"Why am I not surprised to see you brought company?," Ginny noted.

"I can leave if you want me to, Ginny. But I'm here for Darcy. And Tania," Maggie replied.

Ginny slowly shook her head. "No. Whatever I say she'll just pass along to you and it is better that you hear it from me."

"So, why don't you start by explaining what possessed you to cast a spell that summoned spirits?" I let the pun hang in the air between us and I thought I caught the edges of Ginny's lips quirk into the hint of a smile.

"You may not know that my family can trace its roots all the way back to the Witch Trials in this area."

"Tania had mentioned it to me once," I confirmed.

"Well, even with all of that history, the connection to this place, sometimes it feels a little empty. My parents didn't really talk about our ancestors. And ever since I was a teenager and my magic revealed itself, I wanted to know that history. It was almost like a compulsion. For a while I found ways to ignore it, but this year, it's been consuming me."

"So, you found a way to connect with those ancestors you were so curious about." In a way, I could understand her interest. I still had unanswered questions about my own heritage—the way magic ebbed and flowed in my family.

"I found this old book of spells in my basement a couple of months ago," Ginny admitted. "I knew that the veil between the world of the living and the dead is thinnest at this time of year. And once I convinced Rick to bring back the bonfire, I knew I had the perfect place to do it."

"Did he know what you were planning?" Maggie interjected.

"Not entirely. He knew I was looking. He warned me it could be dangerous and I promised I wouldn't do anything risky."

*I'd say that plan backfired.*

"I thought I knew what was going to happen. I just wanted to talk to them, to understand what it was like for them. I wanted to know how our family managed to stay so strong even when we lost members to the trials."

"You couldn't just read family diaries?" I quipped.

Ginny fixed me with an irritated glare. "I didn't think it would go wrong. I thought I'd summon them, we'd chat by the firelight, and then at midnight their spirits would cross back over into the land of the dead."

"Clearly that didn't happen," I pointed out. "Obviously."

"So, do you have any theories on what happened?" Maggie leaned the left side of her body against the nearby wall. I watched as the fabric of her jacket rippled and Beau appeared.

"Honestly, I don't know. I thought I followed the spell to the letter, but then Darcy coming out as a witch ... Maybe I was a little distracted and the next thing I knew, they're gone."

"You're blaming me?" I snapped.

"No. I'm just saying, I think my attention was divided."

"What do you mean 'and then they were gone?' Did you see or speak to the spirits?"

"For a minute or two, I could see them swirling in the flames. I could make out three distinct faces. But before I could even introduce myself, the one in the middle got really angry and then they sort of flew out of the fire and disappeared."

"We saw them leave the fire, too," Maggie said. "But it looked like they went straight into Tania. And I'm guessing Vinnie and Rick, too."

"But why them?" I mused.

"I don't know," Ginny replied, gazing toward her

shoes. "I hoped that maybe I was wrong and Rick wasn't affected."

"Tyson said he saw Rick run off into the woods with no clothes on," Maggie said.

Ginny's head snapped up so she met Maggie's gaze. "He did what?"

"Seems he's gone streaking," I reiterated.

"Oh, that is not good."

"Is there somewhere we can go to try and sort this out? Maybe we ought to see the book you used. It might explain what happened," I suggested.

"I can't leave Vinnie alone. He doesn't know what he's doing and he could get hurt."

"Bring him along, then. It's got to be better than sitting shackled to a tent pole."

"You saw that little stunt this morning. What else did you expect me to do?"

It was a fair point and I tried to put myself in her shoes. I'm not sure I would have done any different. Maggie held up her tablet. "We may not need to go looking at Ginny's book, remember?"

"We've got a copy here. If you can show us which one you used, maybe we can start finding a way to reverse it."

"It's worth a try," Ginny said.

Maggie turned the device on and handed it over

to Ginny. Ginny swiped through the first few pages, trying to find the spell she'd used. She finally turned it back around so that we could see it. I bent down to read the small explanation at the top of the page.

**Ancestral Summoning Spell**

To be used only by full blood relations.

"You're sure you're a full blood relation to these people?"

"Yes."

"I mean it's possible you aren't though. Maybe that's why it went sideways."

Ginny shook her head. "I'm telling you, I am. I've got a family tree I can show you to prove it."

Maggie flipped through the text on the screen. "I'm not seeing anything else that might make things go wrong. I mean there's one spot that mentions the channel for connection shouldn't be left open indefinitely. But it doesn't sound like you did that."

"Could casting it so close to Halloween have been the problem?" I wondered.

"Weren't you listening, I told you I did it now since it would make things easier."

"Yeah, but what if that barrier was supposed to keep them at bay for a reason? What if they were stronger than you expected and they just did whatever they wanted?"

"Were they killed during the trials?" Maggie tucked the tablet back under her arm.

"Yes, they were burned at the stake. Other relatives managed to escape and came back when the fervor had died down."

"So, they'd be pretty angry at the world and to be brought back in fire seems as if it might rub salt in those wounds," I said.

"Okay, so maybe I did piss them off. I still don't see how that's going to help us," Ginny muttered.

If I was being honest, I wasn't sure how it helped either. It just felt like it should have been pointed out.

"Do you have any idea why they would have chosen Tania, Rick, and Vinnie to possess?" Maggie asked.

"No."

As we stood in the back alley, a disturbing thought dawned on me. "What if the why isn't as important right now?"

"What are you talking about?" Ginny's tone took on a hint of a whine.

"Earlier when I went to your booth and talked to Vinnie, he looked confused when I called him by his name. When I flat out asked him his name, he told me it was Agatha."

"What?" Ginny's eyes widened as she spoke.

"Sam said ..." I paused, unsure of whether Ginny knew of Sam's existence. "Uh, he's the ghost that haunts the B&B."

"I've seen him in passing," Ginny replied.

"Well, he's keeping an eye on Tania for us and he told me that she said some not very nice things to him. But the way she spoke didn't sound like Tania. Yet it was as if she still had Tania's memories."

"What if the spirits are in the driver seat? Meaning that the real people are still in there somewhere waiting."

"We just have to get them to wake up."

But that posed a new question. How in the bloody hell did we manage that?

"We need to get them all in one place, so we can keep track of them," I said.

"Good luck finding Rick now," Ginny said. "If he's gone off into the woods, it's going to be nearly impossible to find him."

A distant memory floated to the surface. I stood on Haven Island, seeing through the local vegetation's interconnected web to show me the person I was looking for. I'd been able to use my magic to see the memories of plants more recently, too. It was how I'd seen what had happened to Tania and Maggie a few months back.

"I might be able to track him. As long as we can determine where he went in. I think I can do it."

"How?" Something I couldn't quite put my finger on colored Ginny's question.

"Oh, you're going to see through the plants," Maggie said, beaming.

"Do you even know where Tania is?" Ginny continued, her voice taking on an accusatory tone.

"According to Sam, he found her vandalizing the church."

"She could have moved on by now."

I turned my attention to the chameleon perched on Maggie's shoulder. I held out my arm and Beau ambled over, wrapping his tail securely just above my wrist.

"Okay, mate, can you reach out to Sam? Let's see where he and Tania are?"

*'Looking.'*

There was an elongated pause in my head as Beau searched. I couldn't say that I felt him reaching out with his mind to connect to Sam, but somehow I still understood what the silence in my mind meant. Every day with Beau was a new adventure. After what felt like an eternity, I heard Beau's voice echo in my head again.

*'At the pier.'*

"She's moved on to the pier."

"So, where do you suggest we corral them?" Maggie asked.

"The police station doesn't seem like the best idea. For one thing, Tania already broke out once. And Vinnie, assuming he's still in there, knows all the ins and outs of the place. So does Rick," I pointed out.

"We'd have sort of the same problem with the B&B," Maggie continued.

"And doing it somewhere public like the café feels like we're asking for trouble."

"We can bring them to my place and lock them in the cellar. They wouldn't be able to get out," Ginny finally volunteered.

The resigned look on her face suggested there was more to the story about why her cellar locked like a cell or the fact she actually had one in the first place. She didn't appear to be in a very divulging mood despite the situation. "Okay, so we'll go round up Vinnie and Tania, and then we'll track down Rick," I said, trying to take charge.

"You get Tania, I'll take care of Vinnie," Ginny

said. "I'll leave the back door open. Just bring her straight downstairs."

"Do you really think splitting up is going to be the best option?" I pressed.

Ginny didn't bother responding. Instead, she retreated through the rear door of the coffee shop. Maggie and I were left standing on the street with Beau still wrapped tight around my arm. "Something else is going on," I declared as we started for the alley that would bring us back around to Main Street.

"For someone who traffics in truth, she certainly wasn't serving a lot up," Maggie agreed.

"We're going to fix this, right? I mean, we'll get Tania and the others sorted and back to their old selves."

"I hope so. Honestly, this sort of magic is beyond anything I've dealt with before. I've never confronted the dead. And Sam really doesn't count because he's not malicious. It feels like these spirits have an axe to grind with anyone they come across."

"I'm not sure about that. Whoever is possessing Tania definitely has some strong feelings about the people around her. But Vinnie, I mean ... er Agatha, just seems kind of sweet and a bit lost." Not having seen Chief Hayes since last night I couldn't say what the spirit possessing him might be after.

"You didn't happen to notice if the spell book had a way to banish a spirit from a living body did you?" I asked.

"I had all of three minutes with the book. But it's worth a look."

We'd made it back to the row of booths and were halfway to the pier when I picked up on a commotion in the opposite direction. My curiosity got the better of me and I pivoted on my heel. I grabbed Maggie by the arm and let the clamor of the crowd guide us. It brought us to Ginny's tent. The table was in shambles and Vinnie had disappeared along with a large section of tentpole. Ginny was nowhere to be seen. I heard something clang and caught sight of Vinnie sprinting away from Main Street towards the edge of town that led to the highway, his yellow shawl flying out behind him. For the second time that day his behavior had stopped me in my tracks. We needed answers and Ginny was going to give them to us. Whether she liked it or not.

# 11

"We should go after him," Maggie urged as Vinnie's form grew smaller in the distance.

"What we ought to do is figure out who is possessing Tania and Rick and what is motivating them," I replied.

"You're not wrong, but the information we need to figure that out is at Ginny's house. So, we need to get him there first."

"Right, but we agreed to get Tania. For now, Vinnie is Ginny's responsibility."

As we wove our way through the crowd still gawking at Vinnie's dramatic exit, an idea struck me. Ages back, Tyson had given me a magical stone that allowed me to track anyone. It had come in handy on a couple of occasions and it might just help us figure out where Vinnie had gone. After we found Tania, that is.

"You've got this really intense look on your face," Maggie noted as we picked up the pace towards the pier.

"I was just thinking about the tracking stone that Tyson gave me. It could help us find Vinnie."

"Or Tania."

*'Still on the pier.'*

Beau's words reverberated through my head. At least we were headed in the right direction. I didn't relish the thought of coaxing Tania to come with us and I didn't want to cause a scene in public. But from my brief interactions with the spirit possessing my landlady, chaos and a scene were exactly what she was looking for.

It wasn't hard to find her once we reached the waterfront. The boardwalk was mostly deserted thanks to the Extravaganza pulling everyone's focus. Except that meant this area of town was ripe for destruction. Tania stood about half a mile down the boardwalk, hands raised in the air. Bits of broken signs floated in the air around her. When she turned to face us I didn't recognize the woman in front of me. She had a look of pure glee from what she'd done.

I steeled myself for the confrontation ahead. I needed to decide how I was going to approach her. Would tipping my hand that I knew she wasn't really Tania make things worse? Or would it be enough to catch her off guard?

"What's the plan Darcy?" Maggie whispered as she eyed their friend.

"I don't really have one," I admitted.

"Well you better come up with one and fast. She's got more power than I've ever seen Tania display and it's scaring me."

"We need to subdue her somehow."

"You could chuck pot brownies at her and hope she absorbs some of the mellow," Sam said, appearing at my side. "Also, I don't know what this witch's problem is, but she has got one hell of a temper."

"She can still see you right?"

I caught Sam's insulted look. "She got even more pissed when she realized she couldn't throw things at me." He gestured to a few scraps of wood laying on the boardwalk a short distance away.

"So, she's prejudiced against ghosts?"

"Don't worry, she didn't say anything I haven't heard before."

I glanced at my girlfriend. "Maybe there's a sleeping spell in the book we could try?"

"Given everything that's happened, you still trust this book?"

"Trust it, no. But we've got it and maybe we ought to put it to some use. Just see what you can find. I'll keep her distracted."

*I hope ...*

As if he anticipated the situation, Beau detached himself from my arm and reclaimed his perch on Maggie's shoulder. With an almost imperceptible disturbance of air, he turned them both invisible. It was a trick Tania knew, but we had to go with what we had at our disposal.

Time to throw caution to the wind and hope it doesn't come back like a tornado to kick my arse. I sauntered forward and offered up a small wave. "So, I think we might have gotten off on the wrong foot yesterday."

Tania—or whichever Hayes ancestor was driving her body around—turned at the sound of my voice. The look of contempt on her face made my stomach do flips of anxiety. I pushed through the unease to meet her head on.

"See, I didn't realize who you were. But in my defense you look like my friend."

"So, you believe you know what I am?"

"I think I've got a decent idea of what I'm dealing with. Although I think things might go a bit smoother if I knew who I was talking with. I'm pretty sure you aren't Tania Alvarez, not anymore."

"You mayhap be of some use," she scoffed in a clipped accent. "I still do not grant you the knowledge of my name." It was like she wanted to fit into our time, but couldn't quite let go of her own era.

"Then why don't you tell me about Agatha?" I said, hoping to give Maggie more time to find a way to subdue our possessed friend.

"What do you know of my Agatha?"

"I know she's currently running around in a bloke's body and that's got to be on the weirder spectrum of her existence. She seems kind of sweet. Though a bit too daring sometimes, since she's got another of my friend's bodies under her control."

"She was always sort of simple. They burned her before she could fully explore her gifts."

I watched as Tania's facial features contorted into a look of rage and pain. It was clear this spirit cared deeply for the others she'd crossed into the land of living with. It felt almost maternal. Could we be dealing with siblings? Ginny had said that not all members of the family had faced the same fate as these three. Had that meant they were daughters or sisters or even cousins?

"I'm sorry that she didn't get a chance to learn all that she could do. Believe me, I understand being around people who don't want to embrace your power."

She tilted her head to one side. "Yes, I suppose you do. Rejection by one's family can do more harm than the ridicule of one's neighbors. But do not think us the same."

"You've been angry for a long time and I understand that fury. But why take it out on the rest of us? We weren't the ones who did it to you?"

"You claim to understand persecution and yet you know not the full truth."

"Believe me, it isn't easy being a queer woman of color in this world, let alone a witch. And Tania understands that hardship, too." I tapped my temple and then pointed at her. "I'm pretty sure she's still in there."

"Can you be so certain? She was barely there when first we met. She is weak. Do you believe you are stronger?"

*What? Tania's not weak!*

"Oh come on, it's obvious you're far more powerful than I am. I could never take over someone else's body."

"Now you attempt to flatter me." Her gaze narrowed. "You are stalling, foolish girl." The odd Spanish lilt to her voice gave me a tiny bit of hope that Tania was still in there fighting.

"What would I be stalling for?"

The woman wearing Tania's face raised a hand and with a flick of her wrist cast a funnel of power across the open space between us. I braced for contact, but none came. Instead, I heard a loud, "Oomph" come from behind me. Spinning I found Maggie visible again and sprawled on the ground.

"Petty spells shall not stop me."

"Look, we just want to help you. This isn't your world or your time. You aren't meant to be here. We can get you back to where you're supposed to be."

"You speak the truth, but only in part. This is not my time, but it is the world I should have had. This town is a place where magic lives openly. Where those with the power to wield the elements are revered. This is the time I should have been born in and I intend to take full advantage of all that was denied to me."

There was little chance I was going to be able to

reason with her at this point. And with Maggie out of commission, that meant I'd have to take things into my own hands. Finding my magic was so much easier these days. But I had to believe it could sense my trepidation because it fought coming to the surface.

Come on, magic. I don't want to hurt Tania, just subdue and contain her. My fingers twitched at my sides as I finally connected with the power within myself. I'd been in this spot before, used my magic to root myself and others. The vegetation beneath the water sensed my presence and writhed just beneath the surface. I could hear manic laughter filling my ears, made all the more unsettling because it wasn't Tania's laugh. I did what I could to block it out as I summoned the aquatic plants to wind up over the wooden slats of the boardwalk, eager to secure Tania's ankles. I made a spinning motion with my hands and opened my eyes in time to watch as kelp and seaweed wound around her body like some waterlogged mummy. It bound her feet together and before I knew it, she toppled over backwards as her balance shifted. An undignified shriek tore from my throat as I thrust out my hand, hoping to catch her and break the impact of her fall. The seaweed that had bound Tania bloomed beneath her, cushioning her landing. She glared at me as the kelp wrapped around her mouth like a gag.

I bent over the older woman. "I really am sorry for all of this. I just want my friend back. It's nothing against you."

For the time being, I made sure the vegetation kept her securely confined on the boardwalk. She struggled halfheartedly against her bonds, but I had to trust that she wouldn't get free. I rushed to the other side of the pier and fell to my knees at Maggie's side. Beau lay curled up on her chest and I watched him bob up and down as she breathed.

*At least she was still alive.*

"Maggie, you need to wake up. Come on, now. Up you get!," I urged.

I smacked the side of her face as gently as I could until she gave a soft groan and her eyes fluttered open. I pulled her into a seated position. "Ugh ... That sucked," she groaned.

"Apparently, she's got enough of Tania's memories to figure out what we tried to do," I said. "I'm choosing to believe that's a good thing."

"You weren't the one she just knocked out."

"No, but don't you see ... it means Tania is still in there. And if there's one thing that spirit lied about, it's that Tania is too weak to come back. She's one of the strongest people I know."

Maggie allowed me to ease her back onto her feet and she glanced over my shoulder at our friend. "So, any thoughts on how we're going to get her to Ginny's without arousing suspicion?"

I bit my lower lip. We certainly couldn't carry her encased in plants through town. But people wouldn't bat an eye at vendors moving boxes around on trolleys though. "I've got an idea. It's not a good idea, but I think it will work. Give me two minutes."

"What should I do if anyone comes by asking questions?"

I gestured to Beau. "Think you could hide Tania for a few minutes? Just until we get her to Ginny's house?"

*'Will protect.'*

"Thanks, mate."

I took off at a sprint, bypassing Main Street and making a detour to High Time. We hadn't used trolleys to get the baked goods from the shop to the booth. But that didn't mean Sage didn't have one on hand. It was wide enough to accommodate a human body in a curled up position. I also threw a covering over the top just to keep prying eyes away from what it was meant to conceal. I returned to the boardwalk and presented my transportation idea to Maggie with a dramatic hand flourish.

"You want to sneak her past everyone like she's being snuck out of a hotel in a bad movie?"

"Unless you've got a better idea."

I took a couple of steps toward where Tania had been laying. Beau's magic was doing its job. I couldn't see her until I felt a ripple of magic wash over me. Beau materialized on her stomach. I knelt beside Tania, whose eyes were still open, tracking our movements. "Tania, I know you're in there. I need you to hold on just a little longer. We're going to sort this out and get you back to normal."

Tania's mouth moved against the gag, but I couldn't understand her words. I just hoped she wasn't trying to curse me or anything. I ran my fingers along the bonds keeping her secured to the boardwalk and the plants receded enough to allow me to lift Tania up. Maggie appeared on her other side and together we moved her onto the trolley. The plant bindings that had been released from the boardwalk gently latched onto the four supports securing the top to the bottom of the trolley. She wasn't going anywhere. Beau settled in her lap and with a shimmer, they both vanished again. I settled the cover back over top just to be sure.

"You want to swing by High Time's table and load up to make it more believable?" Maggie suggested.

"I don't think we've got the time."

Together we maneuvered the trolley off the boardwalk and back past Main Street. We kept to the side streets leaving the hub of the town behind. Having never been to Ginny's house, I let Maggie lead the way. She at least had a better sense of where we were heading anyway. A stout two-story house rose up before us. If I'd passed it on any other street in any other town I wouldn't have given it a second thought. Its slate roof and eggshell colored siding made it look almost nondescript. It wasn't the type of house I would have envisioned the town's oldest family occupying. There were no cars in the drive and no sign of a garage to park in either. That suggested Ginny wasn't back yet.

"Any idea where we should enter? Try the front door maybe." I asked.

Maggie broke contact with the trolley long enough to try the front door handle. "Locked. Let's go around back. She said the cellar would be open."

I didn't think anyone in town had cellars. I knew for a fact Tania's B&B didn't boast such accommodations. And most of the other houses around appeared to be the same style as the B&B. So, why did Ginny's home have one? We rounded the perimeter of the structure, the trolley trundling awkwardly over the uneven ground to a set of stone steps leading down to a recessed doorway. Leaving the cart behind, we hefted Tania's weight between us and eased her down the thirteen steps. Maggie tried the handle and it swung inward, as Ginny had promised. A sense of foreboding washed over me as we entered the space. Something about it felt very wrong. I groped along the wall to my left for a light switch, finding one and casting the room in a pale yellow glow. On the opposite side of the room were two chains and shackles fixed to the wall.

What in the bloody hell was Ginny doing in this basement?

**12**

———

*I* looked from the shackles to Maggie and back again. The look of confusion on my girlfriend's face no doubt mirrored my own. I eased Tania against the wall behind us and surveyed the small room. It was windowless and boasted a single door leading to the interior of the house. But there was no handle on the inside. Chills rippled down my spine and my stomach sloshed. This felt far more dangerous than anything I'd come across before.

"Why does she need chains?" I rasped.

"I don't know."

"I don't like this at all. We shouldn't stay here."

"We can't keep dragging Tania ... or whoever she

thinks she is now around like this," Maggie pointed out.

Maggie was right. But left to her own devices, I didn't doubt that Tania would find a way to free herself. "Can you, I don't know, give her some extra strong tea or something to knock her out?"

"You can't be suggesting we drug our friend."

"Believe me, I hate this just as much as you do. But you're right. We can't drag her all over town while we look for Ginny and the others. This place looks safe enough."

"But I don't have any of the things I'd need to make tea here."

"Do you have any at the clinic? Or your flat?"

Between us, Tania mumbled something. Against my better judgment, I reached down to remove the kelp covering her mouth. "What was that?"

"You should take all the time you need. I am not going anywhere."

I didn't trust her words. She wouldn't tell us that if it were really true. "You want us to take our time. Why?"

Tania maneuvered the kelp back into place and gave me a smug look. When I turned back to Maggie, she was nowhere to be seen. I hadn't even registered her leaving. I paced the length of the room as I waited, trying to fit the new pieces of information I'd gleaned together. Spirits could take the wheel theoretically speaking, to control a person's body and speak through them. But that didn't mean the host was totally gone. I still didn't know how to expel the spirits. I did know that whoever was possessing Tania was strong-willed and very angry. I'd have better luck reasoning with Agatha, so long as I didn't try to chain her—him—them up like Ginny had done.

As the silence stretched on, another realization dawned on me. I was standing in Ginny's house. She would have a copy of the book of spells she used to get us all into this mess. Tania's display of power had damaged the tablet so we no longer had access to the digital copy. Since they're Ginny's relatives, she should have information about the spirits we were dealing with.

"Small problem, Darcy," I muttered to myself. "You can't get into the house, because it's locked."

*'Sam can see.'*

Beau's voice filled my ears and I looked at the reptile who now sat on Tania's shoulder. I considered his words for a minute, trying to parse his meaning. "He could get in and take a look around, but he wouldn't be able to touch anything."

*'Better than nothing.'*

"Okay. Ask him. But once Maggie gets back, we're going to find Ginny, Rick, and Vinnie."

Beau's eyes closed in exaggerated slow-motion and a few moments later, Sam appeared in the doorway leading from the cellar. He expelled a low whistle.

"Well, well, Ginny has been holding out on us."

"Tell me about it. Look, I hate asking you to get more involved. But could you maybe take a peek inside and see if you can find anything about the people Ginny brought over from the other side?"

"You can't get in without breaking the law, so you're using me to do your dirty work," he said.

"I wouldn't ask if I had any other options."

"You are certainly living on the edge this time, Darcy," he said. "And I'm guessing you want me to look after Tania, too?"

"If you wouldn't mind."

"At least I get to snoop through the Queen Bee's dirty laundry."

"Just the magic stuff, Sam," I called as he disappeared through the door with no handle.

Not knowing what else to do, I crossed the cramped space and studied the chains and shackles. They were made for someone taller than me.

Judging by the scratches on the stonework, whoever or whatever was restrained here didn't like being caged. I swallowed a lump in my throat as I heard footsteps approaching. My heart leapt into my throat as I spun, ready to confront whoever walked in. Maggie appeared holding out a to-go cup.

"It's as strong as I could make it without putting her into a coma."

I took the cup and bent in front of Tania, pulling the length of kelp from her mouth. "I'm going to ask you nicely, please drink this tea and have a little nap while we round up your other relatives. Are you going to be a good witch and do as I ask?"

"You patronize me girl!" she spat. "I will wake before your time runs out. To see you lose every-thing you hold dear."

I very much did not like the sound of that. I held the lip of the cup to her mouth. Surprisingly, she didn't fight me as she drank the tea. She slumped over almost immediately. Maggie looked uneasy about what we'd just done and I didn't blame her.

"Sam's keeping an eye on things. Come on, we're heading to the woods to find Rick." My gut told me that we'd find Ginny with him, too.

Getting to the woods took longer than I'd have liked. Thomas had caught up with us coming back from Ginny's house and he insisted I help with a transaction. The customer was adamant he needed to talk to the 'plant lady.' Maybe Tania's warning about people wanting to use my gifts for their own gain hadn't been so far off base after all. Though I didn't have time to let those thoughts distract me.

"Has it been too long?" Maggie sounded nervous as we approached the edge of the clearing where the terrain shifted into forest.

"I hope not. I mean, the first time I did this it had been days later and it still worked. Only a couple of hours have passed." I glanced up at the sun high above us. It had already started to make its western descent toward the horizon. I pressed my fingers to the rough bark of the nearest tree.

*Let me see what you've seen.*

I closed my eyes just as images started flashing across my eyelids. Too many people and too many days zipped by on double fast forward. My equilibrium faltered and if I hadn't been standing connected to the tree I would have toppled over in a heap. I sucked in air, doing my best to keep my body from revolting against me.

*Not that much.*

The images receded, leaving a blank screen of sorts. This wasn't working how I'd done it before, when I'd tracked McKenzie on Haven Island. I had a picture to work from then. I took another steadying breath and addressed Maggie. "I need a picture of Rick."

"What for?"

"I don't have time to explain. Can you find one on your phone? I need to focus my search."

I heard fabric rustle as Maggie pulled out her phone. I cracked one eye open to find her clicking through the town's website. She tapped the screen, dragging her fingers to enlarge something and passed the device over to me. "Will this work?"

It was an image from the police department website featuring Rick in his uniform, complete with a wide brimmed hat making him look stern and imposing. It would have to do. I nodded and turned back to the tree.

"Okay, let's try this again. I need to find this man. I know he's been through here today. I need to see when he came by here last and where he might have gone. He's in trouble, please I need your help to find him."

When I touched the bark again, it felt softer, more pliable. I focused on the picture of Rick on the phone screen and slowly an image filled my mind's eye. Just as Tyson had said, the chief ran towards the woods. Only there was something odd about the way he moved. It was almost stilted, akin to someone or something who wasn't used to walking upright.

*That's strange.*

He continued forward, his hands clawing at his shirt like it pained him to have his skin in contact with the fabric. Just as Tyson had described, he shed his clothing and I wish I could have averted my gaze. He moved into the thicker part of the woods within seconds and I was spared the full view of his naked form. I took a step in the direction he'd gone and could almost make out his footprints in the underbrush.

"This way," I called to Maggie.

Moving from tree to tree I was able to see the remnants of the path Rick had taken through the wooded area. I couldn't explain why, but I could almost see a path tread through the space, as if someone had traveled this trek many times before. About a mile into the trees, the ground turned rockier and I lost the imprint of his footsteps.

"Why'd you stop?" Maggie's voice rang loudly in my ear.

"It's like he disappeared. I could track his footsteps up to here, but after this there's nothing."

"That's impossible. Unless he climbed one of the trees?" she pondered and did a slow spin, trying to see if she could spot anyone up in the higher branches. "Rick? Are you up there?" she called.

"But it doesn't make sense why he'd take his clothes off," I muttered mostly to myself. "What are we missing?"

The irrational side of my brain tried to put forward a suggestion, but the rational side slapped it down. It was too outlandish even for a town where witches, ghosts, vampires, and spirits existed. Yet, there had to be a reason for those chains. What did Ginny not want to escape from her basement?

I took another deep breath and reconnected with the nearest tree, letting it show me what it had seen. Thankfully this deep into the woods, there weren't too many people coming and going, just animals. I spotted several rabbits and what looked like a fox or two. Only I could sense something larger, biding its time. Though I couldn't quite make out what it was. It stayed on the periphery of my magical vision.

"I think we just need to keep walking," I finally declared.

Maggie didn't argue as we picked our way

through the brambles and undergrowth that rose up amongst the tree roots. We walked on and the sun continued to dip lower in the sky overhead. The farther we ventured, the more I picked up ambient sounds that felt out of place in the woods. I could hear the occasional car horn and strains of music playing. One moment we were surrounded by trees and the next we'd stepped out into a small grove with thick, high grass despite the approaching winter season. I heard the grass crunch under the heavy weight of something as it moved slowly, methodically.

"We're on the far edge of town," Maggie whispered. She gestured toward the edge of the grove. "Ginny's property abuts right over there."

Everything—it all came back to Ginny and her spell.

"Easy now." Ginny's voice rang out in the open space.

Something deep within the grasses growled in response.

Every instinct in my body told me to stay away from the situation. Except my curiosity told my instincts to take a hike. I leaned forward so my fingertips brushed the tips of the blades of grass.

*It would be grand if you could help me get over there without being heard.*

Magic warmed my palms and I felt the grass respond to my request. The blades turned a gauzy bluish green, directing me on a path that would take me to where Ginny stood without attracting attention. Maggie fell into step behind me. She was careful to step only where I did, so the magic protected her, too.

"You know me," Ginny continued as we approached. "I'm not going to hurt you. But you need to calm down. You need to think."

Just then, Maggie and I reached where Ginny stood and came face to face with a full grown cougar. Its fur was thick and tawny. The beast's eyes were eerie with almost glowing rings of amber.

Those eyes, I'd seen them somewhere before. Why were they familiar?

I spotted a pile of clothing sitting at Ginny's feet— men's clothes. The ones I'd seen Rick discard through the tree's memory. The same outfit he'd worn last night when he'd arrested Tania. A lump formed in my throat and as I swallowed, it settled like an icy stone in my belly. Apparently, the irrational part of my brain might not have been so far off after all.

"Want to tell us what's really going on here?" I said, my voice as calm as possible. I didn't need to spook Ginny or the giant cat pacing in front of us, likely sizing up whether it could eat all three of us in one meal.

Ginny didn't look away. "I told you to go to the house. I'd meet you there, remember?"

"You also said you'd bring Vinnie and you didn't," I replied.

"He won't be hard to track down," she answered.

"How do you know?" Maggie interjected.

Ginny pointed to a spot in the distance. "Because he came straight here. He was drawn here ... to Rick."

"To ... Rick?" I couldn't stop my voice from cracking on her brother's name. I spotted Vinnie sitting on the ground, transfixed by the animal in the middle of the grove. He gave a small giddy wave when he spotted me looking.

"You want to know why I didn't trust you when you first came here? Why we don't like outsiders?"

"Is now really the time for a history lesson?" I quipped.

Ginny gestured to the cougar still pacing in front of us. It shook its head, letting out a snuffle as it did so. "He's the reason why we have to be careful about who we let stay in Brookhaven."

"Rick is a shifter?" Maggie whispered.

"I'm sorry, a—a what?" I blurted.

"Shapeshifter. A person who can transform into an animal. They're rare. Like really rare. And I don't think it runs in families," Maggie answered.

"It doesn't," Ginny answered coolly. "Someone did this to my brother. But that's not the point. I've spent most of my life keeping his secret."

Without warning the cougar lunged forward, claws extended. Ginny threw up her arms to defend herself. I could do nothing, standing beside her and watching as the fur melted back into smooth skin. In the next moment, limbs contorted to human shape and Rick fell to the ground at his sister's feet. He blinked up at me with those eerie amber irises before he let out a soft groan and stopped moving.

## 13

---

*I* couldn't stop staring at the man collapsed in the grass in front of me. I replayed the scene over in my head as the giant cat lunged, turning back into a man. I finally had an explanation for why the police chief's eyes were so unsettling. He was hiding something else beneath the surface.

"Help me get him dressed," Ginny snapped, pulling me back to the present.

"Is he safe to touch?" The words fell out of my mouth.

"He's not going to hurt you," she answered and rolled her brother onto his back.

I averted my gaze until she'd gotten his lower half clothed again. Maggie gestured for me to get on the man's other side and together we hoisted him into a seated position. I held him upright as best I could, while Maggie and Ginny tugged his arms through the sleeves of his uniform shirt. Ginny didn't bother doing up the buttons and just settled the fabric against his chest.

"We're going to have to carry him," she announced.

"He's heavy. Can't he help?" I groaned as Rick's full weight pressed against me.

"Nope. He's convinced he's a weakling," Ginny scoffed.

Maggie stepped up behind me and with a swift movement, shouldered his weight. From there, she and Ginny managed to carry Rick's unconscious form between them, which left me to supervise Vinnie. I approached the deputy slowly and offered a hand.

"Hi Agatha, remember me?"

He perked up at the name and smiled. "Yes. You asked my name. No one else has done that. It's quite rude of them."

"Can you come with me?"

"I don't want to leave my family."

"We're taking you to them right now. I know it's

been really confusing today. I think we can help you."

"Oh, that would be nice."

He accepted my offer to help him stand. I kept a firm hand on his back, guiding him forward as we followed the two women with the chief ahead of us down a small incline and through a row of hedges I hadn't noticed before. But when we came out, the back of Ginny's house came into view. My stomach churned as I realized we hadn't locked the cellar's outer door. With no key, how could we have? I urged Vinnie onward so that we passed Maggie and Ginny. I helped him down the steps.

"Oh, thank God," I said with a sigh as Tania's seaweed-wrapped form still lay slumped against the wall.

Vinnie cocked his head to one side. "She still lives?"

"Yes, of course. She's just sleeping. She was very tired from all the, uh, exertion of being alive again."

Vinnie sunk to the floor and curled up against Tania's side. He rested his head on her shoulder and closed his eyes. Behind me, Ginny led the way through the doorway, dragging Rick along. She settled him on the floor on Vinnie's other side.

"For someone who compels the truth from

others, you certainly haven't been telling much of it yourself today," I rounded on her.

"I swore to my brother I would keep his secret at all costs. I'm just glad no one actually saw him change."

"Tyson did. Or at least he saw him run into the woods naked," Maggie said.

"I'm not worried about Tyson."

At that moment, it hit me. The retreaded paths in the woods. Rick had gone there before. He'd changed his form in those woods. Tyson must have known that already, given it was on the edge of his property.

I gestured to the chains on the opposite wall. "Those are for him, too?"

Ginny nodded slowly. "Back when he thought he was too dangerous to be around people, he locked himself in here."

"No offense, but he turns into a giant wild cat. One that looked quite content to eat us. How exactly is that less dangerous?"

"Because that wasn't Rick. Or at least not all of him. He's learned to control the change now."

I wanted to believe her. I desperately needed to trust that the man charged with keeping everyone in town safe wouldn't put us all in harm's way. A lump formed in my throat as I realized I was judging him from a place of fear and ignorance for something he likely hadn't asked for.

"You said this happened years ago. He was … turned. It wasn't his choice was it?" Maggie piped up.

Ginny shook her head, answering the question without words. As much as I wanted to know more, something nagged at the back of my mind. Something Tania—or whichever Hayes relative was possessing her—had said.

"Tania, well not Tania, told us to take all the time we wanted to secure her here. It was like she wanted us to waste time. Which suggests that we don't have a lot of it."

"Or she was just trying to get under your skin—" Ginny replied.

"Oh good, you're back," Sam's voice interrupted the conversation.

Ginny turned to see Sam floating half out of the door with no handle. She glared at him. "You've been in my house?"

He gave an exaggerated eye roll. "Don't worry, I haven't gone through your unmentionables. At least not the mundane ones."

"Did you find anything out about who we're dealing with?"

"You know, I was going to look through this big book of spells until I remembered I can't turn the pages," he deadpanned. "Lucky for you, she left it open to the right page. There were some interesting ingredients for this little summoning spell. She needed objects from the dead to anchor them here."

Maggie tapped my arm to get my attention and then patted her pants pocket. I understood immediately what she meant; the jewelry we'd found at the bonfire. "Like pieces of jewelry that belonged to each of them."

Ginny let out a slow breath. "We'd better do this in the house."She produced a key from her pocket and ushered Maggie and I out of the cellar. Once we were outside, she pulled the outer door closed and locked it.

She led us to a side door that opened into a kitchen, much like the layout at the B&B. But that's where the similarities between the two spaces ended. While Tania's kitchen was industrial and fitted to serve dozens of people at a time, Ginny's was equipped with a small microwave and stove. A squat fridge sat in one corner and a two-person dining table set took up the rest of the space. I couldn't imagine a family living here. But did that mean that Ginny and Rick lived together?

An open doorway led to a hallway next to the fridge and Ginny walked on, disappearing from view. She left Maggie and I no choice but to follow. We trailed her to a small living room with a couch, an armchair, and a table in the middle of the room. On it sat the physical copy of the book Nan had sent me. Like Sam said, it lay opened to a page containing the same spell Maggie and I found on the digital copy. But there was more on her book's page, written in cramped lettering I couldn't make out from this distance.

"I'd like the jewelry back," Ginny said, holding out her hand.

I was hesitant to return the objects. Keeping them might spur her to share what she actually knew. "Tell me about the three women we've been dealing with first. And then I'll give them back."

"Fine."Ginny began to pace. "You've obviously met Agatha. She's the youngest of the family. From what I know, she'd just started to explore her magic when they killed her."

That tracked with what not-Tania had shared with me. I pressed my hand against the bag in my pocket, recalling the other two sets of initials Tyson had found once he'd cleaned the items. "Who are C.H. and P.H. then?"

"Charlotte and Priscilla," Ginny answered.

"So, which is which?" I pressed. "I got the sense that whoever is in Tania is older, and more protective of the other two. Maybe a mother? Or an aunt?"

She gave me a small smile. "You have always had a knack for figuring things out haven't you, Darcy?"

"So, I'm right?"

"That would be Priscilla." Ginny turned back to the table and flipped a few pages farther into the book. A loose piece of paper fell out and she gingerly unfolded it, beckoning Maggie and I closer to the table. As she laid the paper flat, I could see it was in fact a family tree. Just as she'd claimed she had.

Ginny and Rick were at the bottom of it in different handwriting. Clearly someone had kept this up to date. I traced the thin lines back generation after generation until I found Priscilla Hayes, married to a man called Josiah. They had four children: William, Charlotte, Mary, and Agatha. The date of death for Charlotte, Priscilla, and Agatha matched. William appeared to have died as a young child, living no more than three years old. But Mary had lived a long life. Hers was the line I'd traced from Ginny all the way back.

"So, you really are a direct blood relation," I murmured.

"I told you that already. I wasn't lying when I said any of it. And I wasn't lying when I said I wanted to know my family."

"You should have read the fine print," Sam quipped, earning him another withering look from Ginny.

"What's he on about?" I reached to flip the pages back to the spell she'd used.

I squinted, trying to make out the words that had been added to the page. However, the text swam as my vision blurred from the effort. Maybe it was only meant to be read by a Hayes? Marking the page with my finger, I flipped to the front of the book to find an inscription from Ginny's grandmother to her grandchildren.

"I turned back to the spell page and could make out the printed text just fine. But the rest was still illegible. "I can't read it."

"I can't make it out either," Maggie said from Ginny's other side.

"What are you two talking about?" Ginny snapped.

Sam floated closer. "They aren't your relatives. So, they can't see it."

"But you can? Please tell me we aren't related."

"Don't worry your pretty blonde head. We are definitely not related. But I think this magic is only meant to affect the living." He did an elegant spin. "And living I ain't."

"Then can one of you fill us in?"

Ginny pursed her lips as she studied the page. "I might have a way to let you see it."

Without further explanation, she left us standing in the living room. I glanced at Maggie, but she gave me a shrug as if to say, 'I've got no idea what she's doing.' After a few moments, Ginny returned with a pewter bowl, and a small knife. I noticed she also had some alcohol wipes tucked under her arm. I didn't like the look of this.

"I should be able to open up the extra information if I confirm that I trust you," Ginny said, not making a bit of sense.

"I don't like the look of this," Maggie said, voicing the unease I couldn't speak.

"Don't worry, I'm the only one who has to bleed for this." The matter-of-fact way she said it suggested she'd done something like this before.

This was *not* the type of magic I'd been expecting, not even on Halloween.

I watched as Ginny pricked the pad of her thumb

with the point of the knife and let it drip into the bowl until there was a thin layer coating the bowl. She handed over an alcohol wipe to Maggie and I. "Clean your index finger on your right hand. Then put it in the bowl and touch the page with it."

"That's it?" I asked.

"I hope so."

I accepted the wipe and cleaned my finger as directed. It was cold against my skin, but at least I knew I wasn't going to contract anything. I bent over, pressed my finger into the bowl, and lifted it out, trying not to grimace at the tacky coating on my finger. I waited for Maggie to do the same before we both pressed our fingers to the page in an upper corner out of the way of any text—printed or other-wise—and waited for something to happen. Ginny dipped her own hand into the bowl and pressed it to the page, too. She murmured something so softly under her breath I couldn't make it out. But the page fluttered when she lifted her hand and the tiny script sharpened like I'd been given reading glasses and I could see properly for the first time.

"It says here that this spell, depending on the caster's own abilities, could take different forms." I turned to Ginny. "So, how do you suppose your truth magic affected things?"

"I'm not sure."

"I think I've got an idea," Maggie said. "It's clear now that Rick has been keeping a secret, right?"

"Obviously," Ginny drawled, resisting the urge to roll her eyes.

"Your magic is all about truth, bringing out people's secrets. What if it latched on to him, because he had a secret?"

"But I knew what he was hiding. I was part of keeping it quiet. Why would I want to expose that to everyone else?"

"Maybe the spell could sense you were tired of hiding it?" she said.

I was beginning to understand what Maggie was getting at. I thought back to my interactions with Tania. She'd been speaking the truth, too, however harsh it might be. About how people were always relying on her and not letting her feel her own emotions. "And I think Tania has been keeping things bottled up about her abduction. We know she was forced to use her abilities to ease a dying man's suffering."

Maggie's eyes widened. "We knew it took a toll on her. We tried to get her to open up."

"But maybe she wasn't ready to let us know that's how she felt?"

"What about Vinnie?" Maggie began to pace.

"Sam said spirits are usually magical people," I said. "Tania is a witch. And Rick is supernatural, too. What if they're drawn to people who are magical?"

"But none of us have seen Vinnie do a magical thing in his life."

"It can skip people. My mum doesn't have magic even though my Nan and I do. What if he just doesn't have it, but it's still in his family line?"

"And what, he's just been keeping it a secret that he knows magic is real?" Maggie continued.

"Maybe."

"And what if because Ginny summoned these spirits, they latched on to the nearest magical people with secrets to reveal?" I said, feeling a rush of adrenaline at the realization we were finally putting all the pieces together. "But what do these spirits get out of it?"

"Oh, oh crap," Ginny rasped, drawing us back to the book. Her eyes widened as she pointed to a small notation at the bottom of the page.

"If the spirits summoned take on living bodies, this gives them a stronger anchor to our world. If they are not expelled before a day has passed, the possession becomes permanent," I read aloud.

Oh crap, indeed.

**14**

---

My stomach churned at the thought that we might lose the people we cared about. I picked up the book and studied the other handwritten notes, now that I was able to decipher the cramped lettering. There had to be something to tell us how to reverse things. Yet, there was nothing definitive.

I glared at GInny. "You didn't think that bit might have been important to read beforehand?"

She averted her gaze. "I didn't think reading all the added material was necessary for the spell."

"So, does anyone have any idea how you depossess someone?" Sam chimed in.

"Call a priest?" Maggie replied dryly.

"Magic got us into this mess, it's going to get us

out of it," I proclaimed. "But there's nothing here to indicate how we should go about doing it."

"There are dozens of spells in this book. There must be one that will do what we need," Ginny replied, grabbing for the book.

I passed it over and began pacing the length of the living room. "So, we know that Priscilla was the matriarch and she's obviously pissed that her youngest daughter didn't get to explore her powers. But why would Charlotte come back?"

"I don't know," Ginny answered, flipping pages at a breakneck pace.

"We could just ask her," Maggie said.

That drew Ginny's full attention. "You can't seriously be suggesting we wake her up. The last time she was conscious she shifted. We were lucky she didn't do it in front of a crowd of people."

"You have those shackles for a reason, Ginny. You also said Rick can control the change now. So, why keep them if you didn't have some fear that he might lose it and you'd have to step in?"

"I spent years watching my brother chain himself up. I won't do it."

"Then we will," I said and held my hand out to her. "Give me the key to the cellar. And the one for the shackles, too."

"Does it really matter why they came back?"

"It might help us understand what they're after. Maybe we can find a way to give them what they're looking for before time runs out. Maybe then they'll leave on their own." I had a suspicion that Agatha and Charlotte would be more willing to vacate their hosts than their mother. She'd made it perfectly clear that she liked the look of our time.

"I think Darcy's plan has merit," Maggie said.

Ginny rolled her eyes. "Of course you do. You aren't going to disagree with your girlfriend."

I wanted to point out that Maggie and I were perfectly capable of having disagreements, but held my tongue. It wouldn't help the situation or get us any closer to a conclusion. After another prolonged minute, Ginny handed over the cellar key. A tiny silver one was attached to the chain and when she didn't offer up anything else, I assumed it was the key to the shackles.

"Go in through the exterior door. It's better they don't see a way into the house," Ginny said as she returned her attention to the book in her hands.

Returning to the cellar, I took a deep breath and unlocked the door. It swung inward and for a second, I paused, listening for sounds of life. Someone's weight shifted as I descended the stairs. Vinnie was still curled up against Tania. My landlady appeared to be unconscious. Rick gave a low moan as we approached.

"Help me get him over to the other wall."

Together, Maggie and I hauled the chief across the small space, securing his wrists in the chains. He could stand if he wanted to, but he wouldn't get far.

"Now what?" Maggie whispered.

I slapped the chief's cheek. "Charlotte. Come on now, time to wake up."

Rick's eyes opened slowly and I took a step back. The pupils were slits and the amber that usually only flecked through his irises was vibrant.

"I don't think that's Charlotte or Rick," Maggie rasped.

She wasn't wrong. The animal within the chief was still on the surface. If Ginny was right and Rick had grown to control the beast, then having Charlotte in the driver's seat must have disrupted that balance. I hoped that this didn't mean the chief's hard earned control would be gone once we got him sorted out again.

"Take it easy," I said, holding my hands up in a placating gesture. "I just want to talk to you. Can we do that?"

Rick's arms pulled against the chains, testing out

their range of motion. He bared his teeth and let out a guttural growl.  I took another step back just in case he tried to lunge. I had no idea how strong he was with the animal so close to the surface.

"Charlotte, be calm. She is nice," Vinnie said.

"Listen to your sister. I don't want to hurt you. I just want to understand what brought you all here."

Maybe Agatha would have some idea of why her sister was called here by Ginny's spell. I pivoted so I could keep them both in my field of vision. "Maybe you can help me, Agatha. I understand why you came back. I know you barely got to use your magic. But what about Charlotte?"

Vinnie's jaw worked as the spirit within him toyed with whether to answer my question or not. He cast a look down at Tania, as if asking permission from the woman within. When he didn't get it, he looked back to Rick.

"I should not speak of it."

"It's okay. I told you we want to help you. But we can't do that if we don't understand why you three specifically came here."

"It was so cruel of them, the townspeople. Charlotte was different. She could see things yet to come and they resented her for it."

*She'd had visions like Nan.*

"She said once that we would lose everything. But a chance would come when we could be free of the oppression and the pain."

I blinked, processing Agatha's words. "She saw this coming? She knew you'd get pulled from death into living bodies?"

She nodded slowly. "I did not understand her words then. But I do not doubt the truth of her sight now."

"You know you can't stay here," Maggie interjected.

"But why not? It was foretold."

"Have you seen the bodies you and your sister are in?" I asked.

"I did wonder at the strange feelings between my legs."

"You two are trapped in the bodies of men. Grown men. You can't possibly want to stay like that."

From behind me, I heard a snarl turn into a laugh and glanced at Rick to see him throwing his head back, teeth bared as his whole body shook from the gesture. "We could just take yours," he finally said.

"Look, you've had your fun romping around our time. but you're not supposed to be here. I don't know what you saw in your visions, but it wasn't taking over my friends' bodies permanently."

"You aren't strong enough to stop us, little witch," he spat. He nodded toward Tania. "You are going to wake her."

"I think I'm happy to have her sleeping, thanks."

"No, my sister has seen it," Agatha said.

I looked at Maggie. This wasn't the type of information I was hoping for, but at the least I knew we couldn't wake up Tania. Not until we could be sure the spirits had been banished back through the veil.

"Our blood runs deep in this place. We are rooted here, like a tree left to grow for years and years. We are a part of it. You can never get rid of us," Charlotte continued. "You are the one who does not belong here. This is not your place. And you will never take root."

"Hate to burst your bubble, but I've already rooted. And you really shouldn't make plant puns to a hedge witch."

I held a hand out toward Tania and the kelp that had kept her gagged slithered off her face and shot across the room, wrapping around Rick's mouth. Just then, Sam's head came through the wall. "You need to get in here. Ginny's found something."

Maggie disappeared up the stairs, leaving me

alone in the room for a moment. I cast a glance over each person in turn. "I'm going to find a way to free my friends," I declared and started for the door.

Vinnie rushed forward, throwing his arms around me in an impromptu hug. I tensed at the gesture. He held me tight for a moment. "Yes, you are going to try so very hard," he whispered in my ear.

I managed to push him away and follow Maggie up the stairs, pulling the door shut behind me. When I reentered the house, I found Maggie and Ginny standing side by side in the kitchen.

"What'd you find?" I asked.

"Hopefully a way to get these witches out of our friends," Ginny answered.

"Did you know that Charlotte could see the future?" I noted. "She apparently saw this coming all those years ago. They've spent centuries waiting to be pulled back to the land of the living."

"She also seems pretty confident we aren't going to figure this out in time," Maggie said.

"Not even people who see the future are infallible. Just because she saw they were coming here doesn't mean they know exactly what's going to happen."

"I suppose I could make some more tea like we

did with Tania. Just knock the other two out," Maggie suggested.

Ginny's blonde hair bobbed as she shook her head. "We're going to need them all conscious for this."

"What are we doing exactly?" I peered over her shoulder at the page open on the counter.

**A Spell to Reject Unwanted Spirits**

Underneath it was a list of ingredients, mostly herbs and some tinctures I didn't recognize. The explanation of the spell indicated it was meant to expel spirits from a specific place.

"This sounds like it's to keep them out of your house. Not get them out of a person's body."

"It's the closest thing I could find," Ginny snapped.

"It might still work. If we can cast it on a small enough place while they're in it, then maybe it will kick them out," Maggie said as she ran her finger down the list of ingredients. "I think I've got some of these back at the clinic."

"Get them. Darcy and I will work on the plant side of things."

Charlotte's words echoed in my head: "You are not strong enough, little witch."

"I don't think Charlotte counted on Maggie or you being pulled into this."

"What do you mean?"

"She told me I'm not strong enough to stop them. And I mean, she's probably right. On my own, I couldn't do any of this stuff. I've never cast a spell like this in my life. But you have. And Maggie understands tinctures and that kind of stuff, and me, I know plants."

"She knows we're working together now," Ginny pointed out.

"Yeah, but I think she's been so focused on actually getting here that I don't think it's fully registered that they're facing off against three witches."

"Well, let's hope it stays that way. Since I think this is going to take at least an hour to simmer and reach the consistency we need."

I looked at the clock on the stove. It was almost two o'clock in the afternoon. She'd summoned them closer to nine or ten o'clock at night. That still gave us a small window to work within.

"You know, maybe next time you want to commune with your relatives, you just pick up a phone and call the ones who are still alive," I proposed.

"I get it, okay? I screwed up," Ginny sighed. "Rick

warned me about meddling in this sort of thing. I don't know if he sensed that something would go wrong or what, but he never wanted me diving into the deeper parts of magic. The type of stuff that could really change reality."

"I think he was just trying to protect you. He's your brother and it's his job."

"He's not always been against magic. I mean, he had some talents himself. I think that might be why he ended up becoming what he is."

"I thought you said someone made him this way."

'They did, but he always had heightened senses. Being a shifter just brings it to a whole different level. But ever since then he's always told me I should keep my magic as low key as possible ... make myself integral to town so no one wants to run us out, but don't make waves."

I reached over and gave her a swift hug. "I'm sorry you couldn't practice your gifts as openly as you wanted."

She didn't shy away from the embrace. "Maybe that's why I felt like I needed to connect with these women specifically. Because they knew what it was like."

"I hate to tell you this, but your relatives are kind of awful."

She let out a soft laugh. "Yeah. Seems they are."

"So, what sort of plants do we need?" I released my grip on Ginny and turned back to the book.

"Some sage, rose petals, and something to anchor them to death."

"Oh, like orchids?"

"Yeah, that could work. But I don't know where we're going to find them."

There was a florist off Birch Street. Though I suspected they had a limited supply at the Extravaganza. But maybe we didn't need those.

"If I have something to start from, something bland, then maybe I can grow them."

"Bland?"

"Uh, not the right word. Like the other night at the bonfire. I made roses and other flowers bloom from the grass. They don't normally do that, but I was able to coax them out. What if I could do that again?"

"Feel free to use my back yard."

"How much of it do we need?"

"As much as you can make."

"And where are we going to try and expel them?

It needs to be confined enough that they'll leave their hosts to escape."

"We'll take them back to where it all started. It's away from people and we shouldn't be interrupted."

Something nagged at the back of my mind, a warning that a piece of our plan might not work. But I couldn't put my finger on what it was. So, I headed back out into the yard, ready to try my hand at growing some flowers from grass again. I never would have thought this sort of thing would be possible a year ago. And now the prospect of making something new, transmuting another plant thrilled me.

I was about to settle in the lushest part of the yard, where I wouldn't have to dig so deep magically speaking, to get the grass to grow when I noticed an odd shadow on the ground. I turned to see the door to the cellar stood ajar. My heart stopped and my body froze in place. Panic squeezed the air from my lungs until little black spots popped in my vision.

Finally, I sucked in a breath. My legs lurched forward and carried me down the steps. The cellar was empty save for the wide strands of dried kelp and seaweed that littered the floor. Our friends were gone.

# 15

———

I reached for my pocket, hoping to find the keys Ginny had given me. They were gone. I swallowed as I realized exactly what had happened. The hug—it hadn't been a gesture of anything positive. Agatha had used Vinnie's police skills to pick my bloody pocket. I ran back up the steps and around the side of the house.

"They're gone!" I yelled through the open door.

Ginny stuck her head out from the kitchen. "What do you mean they're gone?"

"I mean, Vinnie, or Agatha, oh I don't even know anymore, picked my pocket and must have freed Charlotte. And they unbound Tania, or Priscilla."

Ginny's jaw worked like she wanted to say something, but thought better of it. When she spoke, she did so through gritted teeth. "We'll just have to hope they haven't gone far." She pointed to me. "You still need to get those flowers, now."

Part of me wanted to protest at her direction, but she was right. Finding them wouldn't do us any good if we weren't prepared to banish them back to the realm of the dead. My palms were slick with sweat and my fingers trembled as I returned outside to the patch of grass that still swayed in the breeze. I settled cross-legged and dug my hands into the earth.

"I know this is going to sound mad, but I need to change what you are. I know you are grass and that's all you ever expected to be, but it isn't what you're meant to be now."

The ground warmed beneath my touch as my magic bubbled to the surface, covering me from head to toe in a thick coating of power. I gave a sharp inhale as my fingers sunk deeper into the ground, as if I were putting down roots of my own. The actual plant roots wound around my knuckles, holding fast.

"Okay, let's try making some sage," I murmured.

That felt like the easiest part. After all, it was closer to grass than either a rose or an orchid. In my mind's eye, I pictured the grass twisting and stretching to become a sage plant. I felt something soft brush against my knee and when I opened my eyes, a sage plant sprawled against my pants.

"That wasn't so bad," I said, feeling confident.

The roses and orchids proved to be harder to conjure, even though I'd done it so easily the night before. Maybe my own fear was holding me back, but it took a solid ten minutes just to get a single orchid bloom to materialize.

"How's it going out there?" Ginny called, breaking my concentration.

"Brilliant," I said, sweat beading on my brow.

"I think I found everything we need," Maggie's voice floated in from my right.

"Still working on the plants," I said. "Oh, and they escaped."

"Then we better work fast."

My girlfriend disappeared into the house, leaving me to finish changing grass into flowers. By the time she and Ginny reappeared, I'd managed another three or four blooms along with a dozen roses. My arms felt heavy and the rest of me wanted to collapse. Only I didn't have time to give in to the exhaustion.

"This still needs an hour to brew," Ginny said as I handed over what I'd grown.

"Maybe we should try and lure them back to

Tyson's then? Meet you there?" I said, my words coming out sluggish from the exertion.

"I don't like the idea of splitting up again," Maggie said.

"But Darcy's right, we might not have a choice. If they leave town, then we are screwed," Ginny replied.

Something about leaving town stuck with me. "I don't think they want to leave town."

"But Tania was out of town the first chance she got. I mean Priscilla was," Maggie reminded me.

"But I don't think she would have gone for good. Not without her daughters. And Charlotte said something to me about them being part of this town, rooted here by centuries of blood. I think they see this as their home and they aren't keen to leave it."

"So, what do you think they're up to then?" Maggie asked.

"They want people to know they're here to stay. Both Priscilla and Agatha were making mischief at the center of town, where they could have the biggest audience. I think maybe if Rick didn't have so much control over the animal within he would have shifted in public, too," I surmised. "I think we'll find them at the Extravaganza."

"Then that's where we head."

"Just be careful. They've proven they're cunning. And they still have our friends' memories," Ginny said. "They can use that against you."

"We'll be okay. Just get the concoction ready and meet us at Tyson's," I said and allowed Maggie to drag me to my feet.

I took a step toward the front of the house and faltered. Maggie moved to let me lean on her, but I shook my head. "I'm okay, I just remembered, we'd left Beau with Tania. I didn't see him down in the cellar when I looked though."

"He's not here," Sam's voice filtered out from the kitchen. "They took him."

"You saw them go and you didn't let any of us know!" Ginny snapped.

"I sensed him leave. I didn't see them break out," he corrected. "I don't think they'd hurt him."

If they tried, there'd be hell to pay. I closed my eyes. *'Beau, if you can hear me, we're coming for you.'*

*'Hurry.'*

The note of fear in Beau's response made my heart hammer against my breastbone. He'd heard me. That was a good sign. But that also meant he'd probably been searching for me, too. I gripped Maggie's hand and walked around the front of

Ginny's house. Time to put some old witches in their place.

THE SHOUTS WERE a good indication of where our missing possessed friends had gone. I tried to make my body move faster, but it was like trying to walk through setting gelatin. Every step felt like a huge effort and I was certain I wouldn't make it. Then, I felt Maggie's hand press between my shoulder blades and a rush of energy raced down every nerve ending, setting my muscles and joints on fire. When the sensation subsided, I felt like I'd had a full night's rest and even a decent meal or two.

"How long have you been able to do that?" I asked Maggie as we picked up the pace, falling into a sprint side by side toward Main Street.

"You forgot what I did the day we met?" she asked, her breath coming in more ragged gasps than I'd like.

I remembered how her hands had warmed against my skin, taking away the aches from the fender bender. "Remind me not to ask you to do anything like that again for a while."

"I'll be fine."

The shouting got louder as we approached and I could see people beginning to run in all directions. Definitely not a good sign. I heard a crash and skidded to a halt in time to see what was left of Ginny's booth, thanks to Vinnie's earlier escape, go crashing to the ground. Coffee spilled onto the street. Priscilla through Tania's eyes spotted me and offered a contemptuous look. Without the fur wrap, she flaunted Tania's exposed shoulders. She'd even managed to make the slit in the dress more revealing. Priscilla was embracing the twenty-first century's beauty standards and it made my stomach churn.

"You thought you could silence me, just as they tried."

"It really isn't personal," I called.

"We need to get them out of here," Maggie said in my ear.

"Any suggestions?"

"Not a clue."

I scanned the crowd trying to find Vinnie and Rick. Maybe they'd be able to convince Tania to go with us without making such a scene. We heard more shouts down the street and I pushed past Tania to find that Vinnie was once again airborne. He seemed to have gained even more control over the ability as he launched high off the ground. Every now and then he'd wave his hand and send objects around him skyward. Bits and bobs from nearby booths, and even people's purses and cell phones.

"I'm not going to catch you this time," I called up.

"I no longer require your help."

"I'll admit, you got one over on me with that hug. I didn't even feel you lift the keys."

That drew his attention and he floated back down to ground level, the flower petals and shawl fluttering in the breeze. "I did not like deceiving you, but I knew it had to be done. You could not leave my sister chained like an animal or my mother subdued in such a manner."

"If you lot had vacated the premises of your own accord, none of that would have been necessary."

He cocked his head to the side. "You know, it is fascinating. This body wanted so much to feel the gifts I have. The moment he recognized I could give him what he never had, he relinquished control. I do not think he wants to be just himself anymore."

"See, now you've left us no choice but to kick you out."

"I did tell you that I knew you would try your very hardest. I am sorry it will not be successful."

"Oh, so you've gained some clairvoyance now, too?"

"No, but I have seen that we will be victorious," Charlotte responded in Rick's voice from behind me. "I think it is time we remove these obstacles." They'd clearly had enough time for a wardrobe change. Charlotte in Rick's body now sported jeans and a tight black t-shirt.

"I resent that, thank you very much."

I heard more things crashing as Priscilla moved down the street, sending tables toppling over. A group of little kids dressed in an array of Halloween costumes huddled together, clearly confused by what they were witnessing. I needed to clear the area. It looked like they weren't going to let us lead them to the clearing on Tyson's property.

Taking a chance, I pushed my way past Vinnie and headed into Ginny's café, spying a bullhorn laid on the counter. Almost like someone knew it might come in handy. I scooped it up and returned outside.

"Everyone, we need you to please leave Main Street for the time being. We're really sorry for the disruption. We just need to get some things in order and everything should go back to normal," I said, my voice amplified by the microphone.

Only no one moved. In fact, they'd all gone

statue-like. All except for Maggie who now found herself tied to a barren tentpole with what looked like coarse rope.

"My daughter told you that you would not be strong enough to stop us," Tania's voice called, as if goading me to engage.

I was getting really tired of hearing this woman's hatred spewed from my friend's mouth. "And I keep telling you that we don't want to hurt you."

"Yet you want to banish us from this world," she scoffed.

"You don't belong here. You had your time. I'm sorry it was horrible and everyone was right prats to you for having magic. And probably for being women on top of it. But that's not our fault and this is our time."

"Not any longer. We are going to make this town what it should have been all along. Ours."

"You think scaring people is going to get you anywhere? You aren't Tania Alvarez. If you were, you'd be able to sense their fear. And it would break your heart, knowing they were terrified of you."

"Your precious Tania is not here anymore."

"I think she is. You could have done a lot more damage, you could have hurt people, but you didn't. Now maybe you'll say that you don't actually want to hurt anyone, but I believe Tania's in there and she's keeping you at bay."

"She will be gone soon enough."

"And you'll say that Rick is gone, but he kept you from hurting people, too," I addressed Charlotte. "You didn't see that coming, did you? It's got to be a lot harder trying to keep more than one person in check inside there."

"You stall again, child," Priscilla shouted. She held out her hands and like magnets, Vinnie and Rick appeared at her sides. She took their hands and an intense wave of power hit me, knocking me down. "We will remove you from this place as they should have done the moment you came here."

"That's enough," Ginny's voice rang out. She marched down Main Street, a tiny jar tucked under one arm. "I brought you here all because I wanted to understand my heritage. You were bitter and angry. I am sorry that I ever tried to communicate with you. Because you are not the legacy this family left."

"You think you are a better reflection of this family?"

"My brother and I protect this place. We make it safe for people like us to have a place to exist, to belong without fear or ridicule. We are the Hayes that made this town, not you. And it is time for you to go back from where you came."

She twisted the top off the jar and lobbed the contents at the trio standing in the middle of Main Street. The jar shattered on the ground and the concoction splattered on what looked like a translucent barrier. They were using their collective power to cling to this world. They wanted to be a part of this place so badly. Only then a weight shifted in my pocket.

*'Bind them.'*

Beau's voice echoed in my head at the same moment. My left hand dipped into my pocket and I pulled out the velvet pouch with the jewelry Ginny had used to summon them.

*'I don't know how.'*

*'Orchid and her blood.'*

The rejuvenation Maggie had given me was beginning to wear off, but I had enough energy left for this. As quickly as I could I dumped the objects onto the pavement. Spotting the first green shoots I could find, I reached out with my magic, urging them to become what I needed.

"What is she doing?" Vinnie's voice rang out.

"Darcy?" Ginny and Maggie spoke in unison.

"Winging it," I answered and wound the orchid

stems through the jewelry. Then I turned to Ginny. "Sorry about this."

"What—" I picked up a shard of glass and raked it across her palm, drawing fresh blood.

She yelped as I pressed her hand to each object. "I think you need to command them to leave."

"Because that's worked well so far," she grunted.

Maybe the spell we'd intended could still be used. "Just try one more time," I told her as I dipped my finger in the concoction that had dribbled onto the ground.

I did an awkward roll to one side and landed in a bit of fresh dirt. Almost like the universe was throwing me a bone. I plunged my hands into it, letting that feeling of connecting with the earth fill me up.

"I need to protect this place from them," I whispered. "I know they're a part of the town's history, but they need to stay in the past."

"I guided you through the veil to this world and now I am sending you back!" Ginny shouted.

I urged the ground to suck up the potion from my fingers, to spread it to the far reaches of the town limits. I heard cries of pain and when I opened my eyes I saw Tania, Vinnie, and Rick writhing on the ground. Pale wisps erupted from their chests and vanished, sucked into the jewelry on the ground. Finally freed from their possession, my friends collapsed to the ground, once more unconscious. Maggie, who'd managed to free herself in the melee, rushed to their sides, checking for pulses. The fact she wasn't immediately calling for ambulances was a good sign.

I approached Ginny. "I'd keep those under lock and key."

She gingerly slid them back into the velvet pouch. "I think they'll be taking up permanent residence with Tyson. No one else can ask for them. I swear, no one in this family is going to menace this town ever again."

**16**

───────

I had never been so happy to see Halloween pass into the proverbial rearview mirror. The last two days had not gone at all how I'd expected. Yet despite the chaos, I wasn't entirely unhappy with the outcome. I felt more secure in myself, having announced to the world that I was a witch. Much to my great relief, no one had come looking to burn me at the stake, or take advantage of my services. I stood in the break room at High Time, fiddling with my ID as I waited for Sage to return. The cash box from the Extravaganza sat on the bench in front of me, ready to be put away.

"Hey, Darcy," Thomas said as he walked into the room.

"Oh, hey. Have you seen Sage?"

He stopped a few paces away, his jaw working like he wanted to say something. "No, not yet."He cleared his throat. "Look, I wanted to say I thought it was really cool what you did yesterday."

"I didn't do anything," I deflected.

"I heard you and Ginny. If you didn't do whatever magic it was, we'd have lost three really important people in this town. You saved them and us. We owe you."

"Please, I don't need anything like that. This place is my home and that means I'll fight for it, no matter what."

"Well, all I can say is we're lucky to have you around." He offered me a wink, "Besides, I knew there was a reason you were boosting business."

Before I could reply, Sage walked in, a travel bag slung over one shoulder. "Sounds like I missed a lot," she said and beckoned me into her office.

I retrieved the cash box and followed her through the doorway. "I'm not sure how much you've heard," I began.

"Oh, just that things got a little wild yesterday and you had a hand in calming things down."

"I had a lot of help," I said.

"And I heard you made a pretty big announcement at the bonfire, too."

"Did you hear what it was?"

She nodded. "To be honest, I'm not surprised. I could tell there was something different about you and the way you interacted with the plants. But I knew it wasn't my business to pry. I knew you'd share it when you were ready. I'm sorry I missed the big reveal."

"You're okay with it?"

"Why wouldn't I be? You aren't doing anything illegal and you've helped business grow. No pun intended."

Tension I hadn't been aware of melted from my shoulders. "I'm relieved to hear you say that," I admitted softly.

"You can't live in this town and not have some expectation that there are things beyond our control or comprehension happening. You can either accept that there are things you can't always explain or you can pack up and leave. Personally, I like it here too much to bail now."

I held up the cash box. "It's a good thing you aren't pulling up stakes yet, because we did bloody brilliant at the Extravaganza."

"How would you feel about being in charge next

year, too? I'm not planning to be out of town or anything but you handled everything really well."

"You really trust me that much?"

"I do." She looked in the cash box before stowing it in one of her desk drawers. "I don't need an answer right now, but just think about it. You are a part of this community."

"Thanks." I hooked a thumb over my shoulder. "I should get back to the plants."

"Grow something amazing," she replied with a grin.

BEING around the plants felt different now that my secret was out; freeing in a way I hadn't expected. By the time my phone buzzed around lunch time with an incoming call from Maggie, I'd urged the latest seedlings to triple their height and start to sprout leaves.

"Hey, you," I greeted as I answered the call.

"You still planning to meet up at Ginny's?"

"I was just getting ready to head out. See you in a few."

I hung up and gave the plants a small wave before leaving through the break room and out through the kitchens. The walk to the café was brisk as the late autumn wind whipped around me. I spotted Tania's VW Bug parked on the street a few spaces from the front door. I could make out the Public Works employees taking down the rest of the booths at the far end of the street as I walked into Ginny's and found Tania, Maggie, and Ginny seated at a booth in the back. Chief Hayes had pulled up a chair at the end of the table. While Vinnie stood off to one side, gaze locked on the floor.

I took a steadying breath as I approached the group. It still felt impossible that we'd all been through so much in the last two days. I squeezed into the booth beside Maggie and she immediately reached for my hand under the table, giving it a reassuring squeeze.

"I hope you all weren't waiting too long," I said.

"No, you're right on time," Maggie assured me.

"I owe you a thanks for not giving up on us," Chief Hayes said. I met his gaze. Those intense flecks of amber took on a whole different meaning now that I knew the truth.

"We all do," Tania agreed.

"You are my friends. You made me feel like I am part of this place. No way I was going to let anything bad happen to any of you." I turned to Chief Hayes.

"I know things haven't always been easy between us, and some of that was due to ... uh, stuff you were trying to keep under wraps. But I truly appreciate everything you and Vinnie do to keep this town safe."

"It wasn't just that you posed a risk to my secret. Before you came along, crime was low and I think I resented you for changing that." He held up a hand to stop me from speaking. "I realize it wasn't you specifically, but the timing rubbed me the wrong way."

"I get it," I said. I had a lot of questions about how he'd come to be a shapeshifter, but this wasn't the time or place to dig into those details. Instead, I turned my attention to Vinnie who still stood off to the side. "You doing okay, Vinnie?"

He finally dragged his gaze away from the floor and pulled a chair over to sit beside Chief Hayes. "I think I'm going to need some time to work through this."

"Take the time you need," the chief told him.

"No, not that sort of time." He rubbed at his chin and let out a slow exhale. "I've known magic was real for my entire life and I've spent every day being on the periphery, never really knowing what it was like to be able to do the extraordinary. And yesterday, I got a taste of what it would have been like." He sighed. "And a part of me hates how weak I was, to give in to the spirit so fast. I let her take over just to feel that power."

"And that messed with your head," Maggie suggested.

"It's definitely something I need to get my head around."He looked at each of us in turn. "I want you all to know I don't resent any of you for having the gifts you do. I think we're lucky to have you around."

Ginny reached over and gave Vinnie a firm hand squeeze. "I'm really sorry you got dragged into all of this. I never meant for anyone to get hurt."

"I know you didn't. You just wanted to feel connected to where you came from. It will just take me some time. Don't worry I'll get there," he replied.

Before I could add my support for the deputy, his and the chief's radios crackled to life with a call from 9-1-1. They stood in unison and left us in the booth.

"I should probably get back to work, too," Ginny said, sliding out of the booth.

"I know you feel guilty for what happened," Tania said, catching the woman's wrist to keep her from leaving. "But hear me when I say that you did me a favor. I've been struggling with accepting what happened to me this summer. It gave me the chance to confront that. So, thank you."

Ginny's eyes sparkled with unshed tears. "Glad I could help."

She pulled her arm free, leaving Tania, Maggie, and I alone at the table. I was about to suggest we order something—I was on my lunch break after all—but a server appeared with a tray of food we hadn't ordered. It looked delicious.

"On the house," he noted when Maggie opened her mouth to question the gesture.

Once the server moved on to check other tables, I dug into one of the sandwiches he'd brought. Relative silence fell over our trio as we all turned our attention to the plates in front of us.

"I'm sorry I couldn't tell you both how much I was struggling," Tania said after a few minutes.

"People process trauma differently," Maggie said.

"But that doesn't excuse the awful things I said to Darcy ... to both of you."

"Tania, it literally wasn't you saying them. It was the spirit of a very angry woman who'd been dead for hundreds of years," I pointed out.

"Even so, I know I hurt both of you and that breaks my heart."

"Maybe she gave you the chance to say what you

were too afraid to say before," I said. "It was harsh, yes. Maybe there was some truth to it and she didn't just pull those specific feelings from nowhere after all?"

"Perhaps. I just wish it hadn't taken being possessed for me to be able to share those feelings with you. For someone who feels so many things, I didn't want to admit I was scared of what I was feeling."

"You don't have to be afraid. We are here for you no matter what," I said and reached across the table to pat her hand.

"Gracias."

"Let's just hope we don't have any more excitement like this for a while, because I think everyone is going to need some time to recalibrate," Maggie said.

"Oh, it seems that trouble only comes our way every few months. So, I'd wager we've got at least until Christmas before things go haywire again," I said and laughed.

She swatted my arm. "Don't jinx it, Darcy."

"Sorry. I take it back. We aren't going to have any trouble for a very long time."

Both Maggie and Tania smiled at me and I felt like I could breathe easy. The last two days had been exhausting for all of us in more ways than one, but I had to believe it was for the better. Tania looked happier now that she'd been able to deal with the pain of being abducted. Vinnie was on the way to having a deeper understanding of magic and Chief Hayes didn't have to hide who he was anymore. At least not from everyone. Maybe Brookhaven wasn't quite ready for a shapeshifting chief of police out in the open, but I couldn't deny that knowing the truth made me see him in a new light. And the whole ordeal had solidified my relationship with Ginny as an ally. I chose to believe that when trouble next reared its head—and at this point, it was inevitable —I'd be more than ready to face it head on.

## QUICK AUTHOR'S NOTE

THIS BOOK FELT like quite the departure from the rest of the series, but in a good way. When I first conceived of the series, I'd envisioned Darcy and Ginny at odds but less friendly competition and more outright rivals. But as I began writing, I realized it would be more fun to have them slowly grow to be friends. And once I'd made that decision, I knew that this book was going to be a blast to write.

I couldn't wait to have Ginny and Darcy actually pair up to solve a case together. As story pieces fell into place while writing—like the fact that her truth related magic latched on to people holding in secrets—I was so excited that this story was going to be much more of a character piece. I knew these people had things they'd been holding in for several books and it was time to let loose. Plus, we're halfway through the series now, we needed something to shake things up.

I'd always known that Rick was a shapeshifter and that's the secret he'd been hiding and I also realized pretty early on that Tania's ordeal in book 5 wasn't really resolved. But I honestly didn't expect Vinnie to be tied to magic until I sat down to flesh this story out. And Tyson just seemed like someone ethereal we could learn more about.

Speaking of Vinnie, I'm very excited to see even more of him and his magical family coming up. Now that everything is out in the open, I can't wait to see where Darcy's cases take her next. And for a sneak peek at her next adventure, turn the page...

### HIGH HORSE

**It's a race to the death...**

The supernatural town of Brookhaven seems to have settled down after its ghostly Halloween encounters. Darcy and her friends have settled back into a normal rhythm and are ready to celebrate the start of spring with a group outing to the races.

But when one of the horses unexpectedly dies and its jockey winds up in a coma mid-race, things take a turn for the dangerous. In short order, Darcy learns the injured jockey is Vinnie's cousin. She is intent on staying out of it, but when Vinnie begs her to use her sleuthing skills to find out what happened, she can't say no.

Snooping reveals a dark family secret and a cut-throat competition where there is more than meets the eye. Can she reach the finish line before a killer slips away into the cheering crowds?

*Scan the QR code to buy High Horse*

# ABOUT THE AUTHOR

S.E. Biglow is the pen name of *USA Today* bestselling author Sarah Biglow. She lives in Massachusetts with her husband and son. She is a licensed attorney and spends her days combatting employment discrimination as an Investigator with the Massachusetts Commission Against Discrimination.

You can find an up-to-date list of all my books here